TRUTH OR DARE

Kiss or Tell, #2

Danube Adele

COPYRIGHT

This is a work of fiction. Any resemblance to actual persons, living or dead, business establishments, events or locales is entirely coincidental. All rights reserved. Except for use in a review, the reproduction or use of this work in any part is forbidden without the express written permission of the author.

Truth or Dare © 2021 by Danube Adele

Print Edition

All rights reserved.

ISBN: 978-1-7331916-7-8

Dedication

My greatest loves…my husband and my boys.

Table of Contents

Dedication iii

Prologue 5

Chapter 1 15

Chapter 2 32

Chapter 3 41

Chapter 4 59

Chapter 5 83

Chapter 6 101

Chapter 7 110

Chapter 8 119

Epilogue 125

Excerpt: Chapter 1 135

MORE BOOKS BY DANUBE ADELE 144

ABOUT THE AUTHOR 145

Prologue
Simone

Cat and her big mouth.

"C'mon, Simone, don't be chicken. You were dared. You have to do it. Kiss him," my gorgeous friend Seth heckled me. He sat a few feet away in the hot tub, wearing absolutely nothing, next to his equally gorgeous boyfriend, Connor, who also wore absolutely nothing. I, on the other hand, wore my lacy, matching panty and bra set that was now entirely transparent.

Why had I thought this was a good idea?

Oh yeah, because I was a tiny bit shit-faced, and my inner she-beast was running the show. And maybe, in my inebriated state of mind, I'd deliberately been trying to provoke a reaction out of *him*. So fucking proper and respectful all the time. What did I have to do to get a reaction from him?

Topher Merrick.

I'd had a crush on him for the last two years: him and his beautiful eyes that took the time to see into and through me, him and his lean, muscular body that inspired many a midnight fantasy. However, the exact moment I fell for him had nothing to do with his body and everything to do with how he'd treated me.

Our advanced stats class had been kicking my ass a few years back. Math had never been my strongest subject, and I was failing with no hope of doing better. I'd cried on his shoulder after one of our group study sessions, and he'd done all the right things. Comforted me. Told me it was going to be fine. Offered to tutor me indefinitely—which he did for the duration of that class. Was patient in a way that showed the most precious care, something I hadn't felt in so long. Took time to explain concepts, however many times I needed him to, until I finally got it. The only reason I passed the class was because of him.

God, he'd smelled so good. I'd also noted how drool-worthy his muscles were. So calm. Self-assured. Confident. Quiet strength I'd always been able to rely on.

Unfortunately, he'd driven me crazy, only ever treating me in a platonic manner…until now.

He cornered me with those eyes, their color the rich amber of an aged whiskey, and in their depths lurked something new and unnerving: a silent command to prove myself. Confronted with my greatest wish, I sat there in an anxious cloud of self-doubt. Heightened awareness. Raw desire that I couldn't hide.

My heart raced and heat speared my cheeks, but I played it off with my usual façade; a careless smile tipped my lips as though blood wasn't rushing through my veins at a thousand miles per hour, as though my mouth hadn't gone dry as a bone faced with a fantasy coming to life, as though my thoughts weren't racing with a mix of excited possibilities and abject fear of rejection. Yup. It was just good old Simone, acting like she was taking a midafternoon stroll under the bright sunshine with a wide-brimmed sun hat and a fucking mint julip…or something like that.

I shrugged casually. "It wasn't even Cat's turn. She took, like, three turns in a row before Beck carried her off into the house." She'd managed to announce in her anger, at Beck, that I'd had a crush on Topher forever; horrific shock had instantly clogged all the air in my lungs for several seconds just before she'd been kidnapped, shouting threats the entire way. I loved her like a long-lost sister, but damn, what a bitch. And now, Topher hadn't stopped looking at me.

Excitement? Fear? Both? It was hard to differentiate one from another, since the effect was the same: heart racing, cheeks hot and flush.

"Cat was pretty pissed off," Seth chuckled. "Shit.

If any two people should be together, it's those guys. Good call on the handcuffs, love," he added, speaking to his boyfriend. Connor had surprised the couple by shackling them until they got their shit together. They had things to clear up between them.

"We can do without them for a night. I'll stay put, I promise," Connor winked back at him.

"I can't even…" I held up a hand, hot mist evaporating off my flesh in the freezing night air as I pretending to be disturbed by the mention of their naughty kink, though in reality, I was completely titillated. I loved watching. Not them. Seth and Connor were family, not just friends, so it would be weird. No, I was talking voyeurism. Porn.

Porn was my friend, not that I'd ever said that out loud. Then everyone would know what a freak I was. They'd understand why I was rejected by my family.

"Whose turn is it, then?" Topher asked calmly, but pointedly.

He absolutely refused to lose sight of the original thread of the conversation; instead, he'd grabbed hold of it with both hands. He could be tenacious when he wanted. His eyes had locked onto me the moment Cat imploded, tossing those hefty verbal grenades before leaving me behind to face the music.

"You haven't gone yet," Connor offered jovially. The jet fuel we were all drinking had turned him magnanimous, and he gestured with clumsy abandon toward Topher. "You go."

"Truth or dare, Simone?" Topher didn't hesitate. The deep rumble of his voice tickled me deep and low in my abdomen. It always did. I expelled a breath evenly. He still hadn't looked away. If anything, he was challenging me.

The fear mounted above the excitement. Was I fundamentally changing this relationship in this moment? Shouldn't I think this one through? It was one thing to tease, but quite another to follow through, and he was a friend I counted on. I didn't want to end up with those uncomfortable feelings of regret and shame like after every other male encounter I had ever had.

Grouped together for a research methods class early in our grad programs, the six of us bonded over being orphaned in some way or other by our biological families. That's why we chose each other; it's why we were each other's best friends and staunchest allies. It's why we rented a cabin in the mountains every holiday, had a group text, talked multiple times throughout a week. We needed each other.

It was also why my feelings were dangerous. They could ruin what we had going here. Cat's and Beck's issues almost had. We didn't hear from either of them for months because they crossed that friendship line. It had hurt.

My first reaction was to take the demure route

and say "truth" to keep things simple and easy. No fuss no muss. In fact, I opened my mouth to do just that, but instantly closed it again because a moment of "knowing" crept over me. A certain knowledge flashed to the forefront of my mind that this one window of opportunity was a limited-time offer, and that when it shut, it would probably never present itself again. He would think he had the wrong idea and back off, but my need to know what lay in that direction was too great. I didn't want to cower. I wanted to stand with my hands on my hips and tell the world to fuck off if they didn't like me.

I cocked my head. Challenge accepted. "Dare."

A small grin touched just the corners of his full lips; fuck me, he was hot. Butterflies-attacking-me-from-the-inside hot. Heart-pounding-fast-and-furious-in-my-chest hot. Then his smile dropped away again. He said exactly what I knew he was going to say. "I dare you to kiss me."

"Make it a good one, Simone. The guy deserves that," Seth called out.

"Yeah, no quick peck on the cheek. It has to be a real kiss," Connor stated.

"With tongue!" Seth added. They were just being goofy and didn't know how serious I was.

This was going to happen. I was going to do this. I was going to kiss him. I was going to kiss Topher Merrick, and I was going to make it so good he'd never forget this one moment. Forever, he'd remember this one Christmas when we all rented a house in the snowy mountains of Mammoth Lakes, and Simone laid one on him that left him completely undone.

Deliberately, I stood rather than remain under the surface of the bubbles. The water level came to just below my ribcage. Water sluiced down my body, and I knew my bra was not only clinging wetly to my peaked nipples, but it was showing off the goods in their best light. I was blessed with full breasts and a tucked-in waist, giving me a nice hourglass shape I've never complained about. Jessica Rabbit didn't have anything on me.

Unable to help himself, Topher's eyes flicked south and lingered. He checked out my breasts as I took slow, measured steps toward him. Dusky pink nipples topped my pert mounds, which swayed as I moved. He clearly liked what he saw, his expression morphing to one of heat. My body buzzed with excitement.

"I'll kiss you," I said, a coquettish smile in place, but my gaze was direct, grave as a heart attack. I'd imagined kissing him a thousand times. Now I was going to do it.

He remained seated, so when I reached him, my breasts were nearly at eye level. Then he looked up at me, and the desire in his penetrating stare created a fire in my abdomen, sent a throbbing heat between my legs. He was waiting to see what I would do.

My hands trembled only the slightest bit when I

reached out to frame his glasses with my cupped fingers—the specs I'd always thought so goddamn sexy, making him look like a bigger, better, more chiseled version of Clark Kent—and gently set them on the edge of the hot tub. Then I reached out, grabbed two fistfuls of his wavy, jet-black hair, leaned in, and captured his lips in a hot, sizzling kiss.

At that exact moment, I realized this was a huge mistake.

Instant searing heat rocked my world, and immediately I couldn't get enough of him. Blood rushed to my pussy, making it swell with anticipation. Need slammed into me, and I devoured him, feasting on his lips that were so addictively delicious I couldn't get enough. I bit at his bottom lip, then sucked at it gently when he grunted his surprised pleasure. His lips were firm, but giving, and when I licked at their seam, they parted and invited me in.

I barely felt when his hands found my bare ass cheeks, not covered by my thong, and squeezed. I was so caught up in the velvet feel of his tongue rubbing against mine, and the fiery tingles racing along every nerve ending in my body, that I likely helped him grind us together. My aching core sought the thick, hard shaft just inside his boxers, and my soft cry of pure pleasure vibrated between our fused mouths.

"Get a room!"

The drunken shout immediately broke the spell. I'd forgotten we weren't alone. I jerked away, panting heavily, the pulse in my neck tap dancing a crazy rhythm, and our eyes met. His were carnal and hungry, looking at me with a promise. I needed distance, or things would get out of hand fast. He would know things I didn't want him to know, know how depraved I was, how my own family had disowned me. I couldn't let that happen. I didn't want him to see me any differently. It would kill me.

It was then I realized I still had a grip on his hair. Not only that; I was straddling his lean hips, my pussy cradling his steel erection.

"Fuck," I muttered. I let go of his soft locks and pushed off the side of the hot tub to climb off his lap. When his hands dropped from my ass, I felt their absence, a keen loss of intimacy where he had tethered me to him.

"Maybe Topher needs to carry you out of here, too," Connor laughed.

"We don't have any more handcuffs," Seth reminded him, blurry-eyed.

I cleared my throat, turned away from Topher's penetrating stare, and forced my lips to spread in a friendly grin. "Hey, I was meeting the requirements of the dare. Can I help it if I'm thorough?" I couldn't meet Topher's gaze. It burned into me. I could feel it, but I'd lost my ambition to conquer the moment like Wonder Woman, with my hands on my hips. Really, I was ready to throw in the towel for my own self-preservation.

"Now it's your turn, Simone," Seth reminded me.

"Guys, I hate to break this up, but drinking heavily makes Simone a sleepy girl. I'm going to bed." I didn't even wait to see if anyone would protest. I scrambled out the side of the hot tub, uncaring that I was flashing my ass, and picked my way quickly around the patches of snow until I made it through the French doors. I didn't stop until I was in my room with the door closed. Breathing heavily, and with the effects of the alcohol mostly gone, I came to an eminent realization.

That couldn't happen again.

Chapter 1
Topher

That needed to happen again.

Soon.

It was the conclusion I came to the next morning after a restless night of little sleep. Feeling too warm. Having the erection from hell to contend with. Immersed in dirty scenarios that played through my mind where Simone had the starring role.

In one, her luxurious hair was partially tangled around my cock while her mouth worked me over, hot and silky. In another, we were back in the hot tub, and she was straddling me again. Only, this time, we were alone, so I pulled her panties to the side and slid my thick, aching cock into the tight, hot forge between her legs.

And there went my cock again. Stiffer and harder than I could ever remember it being before.

Multiple times in the night, I had to talk myself

out of going to her room to finish what she'd started, but I'd seen her face after kissing me. She'd panicked. But why? It was so good, the feeling so right; then, she'd backed off. I wasn't reading this wrong. The sweet sounds she'd made, the desperate need that had her grabbing fistfuls of my hair and biting at my lip, were the hottest things I could remember. Because it was Simone doing it. Simone.

I wanted to know why she was hiding from this. It was something we could have spent the night talking about—after I'd given us both some relief—but I couldn't go through with it. Partly, she was a little drunk. Sober Simone was the woman I needed to talk with. I didn't want to freak her out when she obviously needed processing time. The other part was that I wanted time. When we fucked, I didn't want there to be any regrets or uncertainty.

So, I jerked off in the shower and went to bed.

All in all, I managed a couple hours before waking up with a start. Early. I heard noise coming from downstairs and was quick to grab sweatpants and my glasses, hoping to catch her alone. It had to be Simone. From the rhythmic sounds and faint moans echoing around the upstairs bedrooms most of the night, something that had added to my own sleepless frustrations, there was no way it could be anyone else moving around this early.

As for my lush sex goddess who kissed like she lived to sin, there was no way we were done with this fuckery. She'd opened that door between us. I walked in. There was no going back.

I went down the stairs, doing my best to tread softly. Not wanting to wake the others was part of the reason for my caution, but I didn't want to forewarn Simone that I was coming. If she heard me, she'd put her guards up, flash me that carefree smile that didn't touch her eyes. I wanted it to be real between us. Honest. No bullshit.

Bacon sizzled on the stove while the scent of coffee percolating seasoned the air. It was a delicious incentive to anyone still sleeping that it might be time to get up, which meant our time alone would be short. I wasn't sure how to approach her; there might be some resistance. Still, I couldn't help taking a moment to appreciate the sight before me.

Beautiful. Fragile. Brilliant.

Mine? If the gods decided to smile on us. Maybe it was time for a Christmas miracle.

Simone was mixing up a batter of something or other, a faint frown creasing the skin between her brows. Her long hair, the rich color of the gingerbread cookies Connor had brought to the house yesterday, was casually tied in a knot on top of her head. A few loose strands pulled away to fall around her face. The loose, petal pink, silky, Japanese-print pajamas did not dim the memory of her perfect tits crushed against my chest, so soft and round and full, and of steam rising off her smooth, sun-kissed skin.

And there was my dick again. I couldn't blame him. He'd been robbed of heaven the night before. Her breasts had been up in my face, inches away from my mouth. I'd wanted my lips on them. My tongue. Part of the self-made mental porn I'd created in the deepest, darkest hours of the night involved paying homage to their perfection.

She wasn't wearing shoes, and her little toes peeked out from under the drape of the pant legs with matching pale pink color. God, she was fucking adorable.

"Your feet are going to get cold," I offered in greeting, my voice sounding rusty from sleep.

You'd think the grim reaper had walked in, she jumped so high and drew in a fish-out-of-water gasp. She put a hand over her chest automatically. "You scared the shit out of me, Topher. I didn't think anyone was up."

"Sorry." But I wasn't sorry, and we both knew it. We stood there, eyes locked for a beat, both of us remembering. Hers flashed to my bare chest and lingered a moment, like she couldn't help herself. Yes, I worked out. I was lean and muscular from the hours I put in most every morning. It was the way I usually started my day. Early gym workout, then breakfast, then work. Her eyes went further south. The sweatpants probably couldn't hide the semi I always seemed to sport when she was in the room. She struggled to bring her eyes back to mine.

On cue, that hand she'd had over her chest did a

quick hair check, trying to smooth loose strands in place with a few quick, nervous pats. Abruptly she stopped, as though realizing what she was doing.

"Uh, I didn't expect...I should get dressed." She set the bowl on the counter that she'd held in the crook of her other arm, looking flustered and out of sorts. I'd never seen her this way. She'd always given the impression of cool sophistication. I was getting a kick out of this side of Simone, and I didn't want her to go start putting barriers up just yet. I wanted her off-kilter a bit longer.

"You're fine. Perfectly covered." I started across the room toward her with a casual, rolling gait, keeping things light, trying not to notice her nipples pushing out against the thin pajama top, but unable to help but wonder if her sensitized peaks were aroused by the soft material or by the sight of me.

She sent a nervous glance over herself.

"What can I do for you?" I asked with a crooked grin.

"Do? For me?" Her eyes snapped back to mine, going deer-in-the-headlights the closer I got to her. I stopped two feet away, noting how her eyes were a blue so pale they looked like the sky at dawn. She was flushed. A little breathless. Off balance. That was the strategy. Then she couldn't hide. I liked that. I leaned a hip on the counter and stared down into her befuddled gaze, noting the color in her cheeks had deepened. Was she thinking about last night? What else was she considering?

"To help?" I said it innocently enough, hiding the grin that wanted to break free.

"Oh. Right. Help." Her eyes darted around, desperate to find something for me to do. "Why don't you watch the bacon and do the toast, or something like that? There's butter in the fridge." Normally, she would have given me a big hug, like she gave to everyone, but instead she just patted my arm and kind of did an awkward friend rub instead. Yup. That was going to change.

I nodded. "I can do that."

"You might need…" She looked down at my chest.

"What?"

"The bacon…" She motioned toward my chest again, her eyes lingering. "It might burn you."

"I'll be all right." I ran a hand over my chest. Her eyes followed. She liked my chest. I wasn't going to cover up. I would be careful, though.

What I wanted to do was shove her pretty ass up against the wall and plow my tongue into her sweet, silky mouth, exploring the taste of her at my leisure. Properly show her my appreciation. What I wanted to do was rip the delicate buttons apart on her pretty, long-sleeved silky pajama shirt with its feminine Japanese branches twined with cherry blossoms and fill my hands with her perfect body.

Instead, I gave her space—but not too much. I

brushed against her, lightly moving past her to get to the stove and check out the bacon, noting how she stiffened the slightest bit. Looking in the skillet, I could see the bacon sizzling away, but it still needed time. She'd gone back to stirring what looked like an egg mix in the bowl.

Her hand resumed its movement at a slower pace while her eyes glanced over at me hesitantly, her sexy bottom lip clamped between her teeth making her look like she was trying to figure out what was happening and how to handle it. She released it, and it slid out, wet and plump. "Thanks, by the way. For thinking of this. This weekend with all of us together."

"I think we all needed it. Particularly Beck." I took a moment to grab the bread out of the fridge and set it by the toaster. "He was desperate to rope Cat into one spot."

"Can you believe they actually got together?" She set the bowl of eggs down again, warming to the topic. She turned the fire up on a skillet that was already in place and tossed a pat of butter in. It began melting instantly. "I can't say I'm surprised they were interested in each other. Joined at the hip for years, the way they were."

We were sliding back into familiar territory, easy conversation. I gave her a half grin that she mirrored. "There were times I suspected."

"When? How?" She poured the egg mixture into the pan and began working it.

"It was there. In their eyes when they looked at each other. Add in they were always together. They understood each other." It made sense to me. They were odd-shaped puzzle pieces that could only fit each other.

"They didn't last night," she smirked.

"Whatever happened, Beck needed her to sit still and listen." Communication was the number one issue most of my clients had. Most anyone. They came to my office, frustrated and ready to throw in the towel because they didn't know how to ask for what they needed, how to achieve their goal. They wanted a different outcome, but they weren't doing anything different to try and achieve it. It wasn't uncommon.

"She wasn't ready yet."

I shrugged. Sometimes, people needed to be pushed out of their comfort zones. "Beck called me up and basically said he was coming. Period. It put me in an awkward position. I couldn't tell Cat. We all know she can be impulsive. She'd jump on a lit rocket without looking to see where it's going."

"But it keeps her feeling safe." Simone's grin faltered as she thought about it. "Her dad fucked her over. It hurt."

"But this is Beck we're talking about." I put a couple of pieces of bread in the toaster. "He'd jump into traffic to save someone he loves."

The skin between her brows furrowed a beat before she said, "Cat doesn't want to be fucked over again. There's nothing like finding out the people you love don't give a shit about your well-being."

"Who? Beck?" I was confused a moment. "He'd do anything for her."

"I'm just saying, I understand her anger. She wants to be able to predict what'll happen to her in a day, and sometimes you need to tell people to buzz off." Her sharper tone alerted me; Simone was taking this a more personal direction. "And sometimes people are just wrong for each other."

"That's true. And no one wants to get fucked over." We weren't talking about Beck and Cat anymore. "But do you really think anyone can actually have control over anything? You have no idea what someone is really thinking and feeling unless they tell you. The only thing you can ever control is your reaction to whatever happens."

Her scowl came out in full force then, and a hint of exasperation touched her voice. "Yes. I understand the psychology of it all, Mr. Therapist. Still, when you get fucked over, it does damage. Maybe you've never had damage done to you, but the damaged person must live with that shit forever. I can totally understand that she needed to stay sane, and for our Cat it meant roaming with the wolves in the wilds of Wyoming through her job with Fish and Game."

"Without talking to Beck first?" My own

irritation was mounting. Normally, I was good at maintaining my calm, professional demeanor, not letting my personal feelings color my responses, but this was Simone, and I had a feeling she was trying to use this conversation as a means of erecting her wall of platonic friendship.

She set the spatula down on the spoon holder and squared off with me, her hands on her hips. "Talking to him would have the potential for confirming her worst fears, and then she would know for certain that he'd done something hurtful. It's one thing to indulge in a fantasy, another to live with the reality of what he did. She wanted to hold on to the dream of him, the idea of his devotion to her, and her alone, a little longer. It makes her world continue to feel normal. Sometimes secrets are good."

"Not for a healthy relationship."

"Some people can't have a healthy relationship without secrets." As though realizing what she'd just said, she looked away, almost like she didn't want me to see what was there, the emotion behind the words. Was there something from her past that she was ashamed of?

"But that makes no sense. By definition, it wouldn't be a healthy relationship. It means someone's accepting an artificial world. Why wouldn't someone want to take the risk? The potential for reward, for finding someone who accepts you for who you are, could be life-altering.

The best thing that ever happened to anyone."

There was bitterness to her voice when she turned back to the eggs and stirred them again. "You make that sound so easy. When people don't accept you, it can be crushing, and you never forget what it feels like to be rejected. Ever. So sometimes it's better to cut your losses and save yourself the pain of repeated slaps to the face."

Was that literal or figurative?

She wasn't talking about Cat and Beck, and she wasn't talking about the two of us. She was talking about a personal experience, and it was painful enough that she was already working to shut me out. It was like a dark cloud had settled over the room. Right then, I realized there were layers, and that even though I'd known her for the last two years, maybe I didn't know enough of the important parts. She had secrets. Now she was putting distance between us. An arctic breeze emanated from her.

Good thing I don't give up so easily. I wanted her to remember what it felt like to be close, body to body. And just like that, as though the gods were intervening to help, the bacon popped, not only reminding me that I needed to flip it over, but spewing several droplets of oil, hitting me square on a pec.

"Shit!" I jerked, more in reaction than from any real pain.

"Oh! Topher!" She spun and automatically put a hand over my chest, concern in her eyes. "Are you all right? I told you this could happen. You should have listened to me."

"It's all right." I covered her hand with my own, trapping it. Feeling her skin on mine suddenly changed my mood. Deepening my voice, I added, "A little hot oil can make things exciting."

Her gaze snapping up to meet mine, she paused, unwilling, or unable, to break away from my stare. Absently, her soft fingers moved over my skin in a light caress, and her eyes slid to my lips. This woman was going to be the death of me. Blue balls. Was that possible? It took no more than a thought for a situation to be created in my sweatpants, much less a touch or a look. Then she remembered herself and tried to step away, create space. Took a deep breath.

"You should flip those over," she murmured, turning to grab her spatula again, her focus once again on her eggs.

"All right."

Deliberately, I stepped behind her with the supposed intention of getting the tongs she'd already begun using for the bacon. They were beside the ceramic spoon holder just in front of her. I let one hand cup her hip under the pretext of keeping her still while the other reached past her for the implement. There was the faintest sound of her breath catching, and her hand slowed its movement, flipping the eggs in the skillet.

"Excuse me. Sorry." I said this near her ear, letting my lips graze it as I crowded up behind her soft warmth. Her silky pants were thin, no kind of layer between us. Neither were my sweatpants, for that matter.

Her breathing was heavier, the curve of her ass nearly pressed against my cock. It would have been easy to lean in, appreciate the feel of her nicely rounded ass on my cock, press my lips to her neck and nibble the flesh there, but I didn't want to push too hard. It was better to keep her flustered without freaking her out any further.

I had an endgame in mind.

At this point, the scent of breakfast had done its job. I heard the heavy tread of feet on steps. The others began making their way in, so I stepped away casually, tongs in hand, to finish my job.

Breakfast turned into a celebration once Beck proposed to Cat. Toasts were given, well-wishes for their future, and further sharing of the new family Beck had discovered, lucky to have been found since he'd been put into foster care. As much as I was enjoying the warmth of the moment, I couldn't keep my eyes off Simone, even though she studiously avoided letting her gaze rest on me for longer than a few seconds before it skittered away.

If there was one thing that could be said of Simone, it was that she didn't like to hold on to negative feelings. She pushed them aside and embraced the joy of any moment. In fact, I couldn't think of a time when I'd ever actually seen her angry or even as perturbed as she was this morning. Was that strange? Was it artificial, or was she in denial? What the hell could have happened to her, and would she ever let herself open up to me?

I wanted her trust. All in. But she wasn't going to just give it to me.

Fantasy. That was the way to get to her. It was the word she'd mentioned. Keep everything fun, a game, a fantasy, and no one gets hurt. It was the first thought I'd had this morning. I wanted to keep the game going, but only between the two of us. We were already friends, and last night had proved we had off-the-charts chemistry. Now I wanted her to put those two thoughts together.

"Seth and I will do the dishes." Connor pushed back his chair and started collecting the breakfast dishes. We'd had a feast, everyone eating far too much, everyone jovial with loud barks of laughter that echoed off the walls, and generally holding on to the holiday spirit.

"I'm getting my ski clothes on. The resort is open today, and I'm going to use it," Simone called out. "I don't care if no one else is going. I am."

"Let's all be ready to head out in an hour," Seth called out to the house in general, likely trying to make sure Cat and Beck were able to hear the plan. With the way they were ass-grabbing all the way up the stairs a few minutes ago, I was going to be surprised if they actually came with us.

"I'll be ready," Simone replied, already turning to make her way back to her room. Trying to escape.

I followed her down the hall and surprised her when I called her name. "Simone."

She whirled around, nearly through the bedroom door. I could see the bed was unmade, the sheets rumpled and looking all too inviting. I wanted to walk her backward until we both tumbled back and wrapped up in those sheets.

"Topher." Her eyes were wide, the vein in her neck jumping. She swallowed, pursing her lips the slightest bit as she did so. Fucking edible.

I tore my gaze away to look back into her eyes. "I wanted to talk about last night."

"Last night?" Her voice hit a high note, a falsetto with a quick flash of a shiny, plastic smile. "What is there to talk about? We were just having a little fun, right? No big deal."

I wasn't surprised she chose to play it like this, but I was ready for it and countered her question with a grin that called bullshit. Moving closer, I lowered my voice. "I think we have a lot to say. Or are you too chicken?"

That caught her off guard. Her smile died and her stubborn came out with a chin thrust. "Not at all. I don't have anything to be afraid of."

"Truth or dare, Simone?"

She laughed but shook her head with disbelief. "I'm not drinking with you."

"No drinking involved. I want you sober."

"C'mon. It was a silly game when we were all drunk."

"Then you *are* scared."

"No, I'm not scared." Her exasperation was plain. "I just think this is silly."

"I'm talking about our own personal truth or dare game. We start it, just between us, right now."

That took her a moment to process. Then her eyes narrowed the slightest bit, and she searched my face—for hidden motivation or meaning, likely—before she murmured, "Just us?"

"We don't tell the others."

Her teeth pulled nervously at her bottom lip, worrying it. Then her eyes dipped to linger on my lips, maybe remembering the kiss in the hot tub, a fire smoking in their depths. Still, she hesitated, her tone a damper as she murmured, "Topher—"

I didn't let her think too much. I moved into her space and whispered my demand. "Truth or dare."

She met my eyes, the fire burning hotter. As

much as she might not want it to be true, this game excited her. It took a moment for her to figure out her response. Almost hesitantly, she said, "Dare."

"I dare you not to wear panties for the rest of the day. Take off the ones you're wearing and hand them to me. Now."

Chapter 2
Simone

My heart crashed against my chest like a wild thing throwing itself against a locked cage.

At the same time, that heavy, throbbing pulse pounded between my thighs, the one associated with Topher's presence. It was a reaction I was used to. One I ignored, usually. But not this time. Kissing him had shown me exactly what I was missing. What I'd missed from every other guy I'd been with.

Combustion.

My body had voted. It was begging me to agree.

But we'd just gotten the crew back together after Cat and Beckett made up. Their romance had nearly screwed our entire dynamics as a family group since Cat had taken off for months without contacting anyone.

Of course, it had turned out okay in the end. Here we were. All of us. Their relationship was bigger than their misunderstanding, and it had turned out to be the perfect next step for them.

Not that I thought Topher and I would end up in some cozy happily-ever-after scenario, because that didn't happen for everyone. We were hardly a holiday movie on a cable channel. Not everyone was relationship-worthy.

But what if we did this casually? No feelings. Just fun. Play. I could do that. Live out the fantasy since he was presenting himself to me, but with no expectations? That was smart. Wasn't it?

His eyes held mine. Steady. Intense. Refusing to let me look away.

Was I going to do this?

Was this a smart thing to do?

I took a deep breath. Yes, and no.

My hands shook as they shoved my pajama pants over my hips, letting them pool at my feet in a silky waterfall of material. Still not taking my eyes from his, I gave my underwear the same treatment before stepping outside the pile of clothes. My soft pajama top barely covered my pussy from sight. Only then did I kneel to pick up my panties and hand them to him, a silky scrap of peach lace thong.

He took them from my hand, and a jolt of heat danced across my skin at the incidental touch of our fingers. My breathing already felt heavy when he lifted the intimate cloth to his nose and breathed me in. My lips parted on a silent gasp of shock. Nerves fired. That was so dirty. So hot. Sexy. I could only stand and watch as he tucked them into the pocket of his jeans, then strode off without another word.

He'd just activated my inner sex beast, and it scared me.

It took a few seconds to realize I was standing in the open doorway, partially nude. He'd left me in a fog of lustful thoughts, and it was only after my thoughts cleared that I jumped back into my room, snagged my pajamas off the floor, and closed the door.

The shower was quick. Dressing, however, took several minutes of internal debate. I snagged a pair of undies from my bag, and just as quickly stuffed them back into the side compartment again, fighting the sense of ugly I always encountered when faced with my fantasies and desires. The looks of disapproval and disgust that popped up from memories past; looks that I'd battled internally for several years warred within my conscience.

To sin or not to sin. It was a theme in my family. One that had come with heavy consequences from a young age. Too young. Too cruel.

Like clockwork, just remembering how everything had gone down made me react with an immediate "fuck them" rage. I'll do whatever the fuck I want to do.

When I put it like that …? The were-beast, or in this case, the deviant, came out unapologetically.

A wicked grin crossed my face, and with a smile that felt almost angry or defiant, I slid my leggings on sans panties and tossed my snow pants across the bed, not wanting to put them on until we actually left.

I'd just pulled on my thermal shirt when there was a knock at my door.

"Come in," I called out, expecting Cat. Her stuff was in here, and she'd need it if she was going to get ready soon.

Topher took up the space in the doorway, looking impossibly hot with his white thermals stretching taut across his muscular chest. He leaned against the door frame in a purely masculine pose with his thick forearm braced casually, his black snow pants hanging low on his lean hips. So sexy. Through swoon-worthy glasses that framed his square-jawed visage perfectly, his hot, amber stare drifted over my form. It was like he could see through my clothes.

A shiver spilled down my spine and my nipples tightened. The feeling was delicious and wrong at the same time. I wasn't supposed to feel this good from a look, was I?

"Did you follow directions?" he asked in a voice meant to be quiet. It was low, growly, and his eyes held me tight.

Instead of answering, I asked my own question. "Truth or dare, Topher?"

His eyes widened the very slightest bit, as though I'd taken him by surprise, which gave me a hit of energy. Curving his lips into a sensual smile, he replied, "Dare."

"I dare you to find out for yourself." Even as I said the words, the heat ramped up in my blood, pooling in my secret private places.

Without a pause, he pushed off the door frame and stalked me across the room, his eyes going hot with clear intent. With every step, my breathing turned more and more shallow, coming in quicker and quicker gasps. Then he was in front of me, his hands on my hips, fingers of his right hand digging under the thin fabric of my spandex waistband. Hot against my skin, his fingers, thick and rough, traveled over the curve of my bare ass, sending a shiver down my spine. They continued into the delicate cleft between my legs and ran over the seam of my pussy lips that were softly bare from hair removal treatments over years.

He bent to my ear with his finger still caressing me, giving me shuddering quakes of pleasure that had me gasping when he whispered, "You're wet, Simone."

"Yes." It came out on a puff of air energized with need.

"It seems to me that you need to come."

"Yes."

"Simone, truth or dare."

"Dare."

"I dare you to let me make you come at any point, day or night." His teeth nipped my neck while continuing the touch that was soaking my pussy.

"Yes."

Then he backed me toward the wall by the bed, and at the last minute, spun me to face it. My hands automatically went up to brace myself there, and his hand changed position. It slid around from my ass to push down into my center, cupping the very place that ached with the need he'd created.

"Do you know how long I've wanted to touch you, princess?" His large fingers followed the path of my arousal, found my center, and slid inside me with smooth precision, gently swirling in and out while grinding the heel of his palm against my clit until I moaned my encouragement. But he persisted in his questioning. "Do you know?"

It was hard to think past the pleasure radiating through my nerve endings. "I don't know."

"Since I first saw you in the library two years ago with your short skirt and filmy little nothing blouse that let me see the peach color of your lacy bra underneath." His fingers picked up the pace, so my hips pushed back against him, trying to find his rhythm. His palm almost rhythmically slapped my swollen clit, making me gasp my moans with each breath. He continued, "Then I wondered if you had matching panties on, and I had to fucking work at keeping my dick from getting hard. You know why?"

"Why?" I cried, my hips writhing against him, trying to find his cock.

"Because I kept fantasizing about shoving you up against the stacks and pulling your skirt up so I could see for myself."

He added a second finger, stretching me, the burn a brief sensation that ramped my pleasure just before he curled them inside just enough to hit my spot, and I was slave to his touch, my breathing shredded while I focused on chasing after the pleasure that built with every thrust of his fingers. One of my hands reflexively covered his, almost like I was trying to help him. I rode him. "Please."

"Are you close?"

"Yes!" I didn't care how loud I was getting, even with my door open. My muscles spasmed. Tightened. So close. "Don't stop. Don't stop."

And that's when he slid his fingers out, before I could come, gently caressing and cupping my throbbing lips. "That's mine, princess. Do not touch yourself. That orgasm belongs to me."

"What? Why?" I gasped with angry disbelief, the

fire between my legs raging with desperate need.

"Because I want you to wonder when and if." Then he headed out the door again before pausing, half turning back my way when he added, "Remember, don't touch yourself. Anticipation is half the fun. By the way, we're leaving in twenty. Can you be ready?"

"Twenty?" Coming up behind him, Cat was rosy-cheeked and wearing one of Beck's T-shirts. "Yes. Pretty sure. Just keep Beckett busy until my clothes are all the way on. Maybe they'll stay that way."

"We'll make him pack the gear into the car." Topher smiled, backing out of the room. When Cat bent to grab her bag, he deliberately stuck his fingers in his mouth and sucked—the two fingers he'd had inside me.

My lips rounded for the second time before he was out the door and heading his own way.

"Are you all right?" Cat asked, straightening to see the look on my face.

"Uh…yeah. For a second, I thought I'd forgotten my…uh, my snow pants."

"They're right on the bed, silly."

"I know, right? So silly." I forced a laugh.

Cat was too wrapped up in her own post-sexual euphoria to notice that I was a little off my game, which I was thankful for. At least I didn't have to answer questions that I didn't have a ready answer for. We were able to finish getting our clothes on and our gear prepped, and in short time, had hopped into the car, ready for a day on the slopes.

Of course, while driving the ten minutes to the resort, a delicious thought brought a new influx of simmering heat to concentrate between my legs.

How many orgasms was Topher going to give me before the day was up?

Chapter 3
Topher

There was no going back.

Already, visions of sucking her dusky mauve nipples danced in my head, and we weren't out of the car yet. Simone didn't know the sexual beast that resided inside of me, the demands that would be made.

Would it frighten her to know I had needs that might be seen as atypical?

My muscles felt tense. Ready to claim her. Own her. Now that I'd had fingers moving inside her tight, hot channel, the taste of her pussy on my tongue, I considered it mine. My face belonged between her naked thighs, making them shake with orgasm after orgasm. I could go all night. Ride her until her voice was hoarse.

"So many people," she murmured, her naturally

sultry eyes tracking the scenery out the front windshield as we pulled into a parking spot down the hill. Everything about her fed the fire, but her plump, pink-glossed lips were what grabbed my attention once I shut off the engine and glanced over at her. She had a corner of her bottom lip absently clamped between her teeth. It was my plan to bite and suck that lip before long, then see her pretty lips circling my thick cock.

"It is the holidays, Baby-cakes," Connor announced, interrupting the erotic vision playing out in my mind. I let out a deep breath. Getting out of my SUV with an erection was not cool. I had to be patient, and I knew this, particularly, when I saw the joy on Connor's face. In his enthusiasm, he bear-hugged Simone from his place behind her in the back seat. "C'mon! Let's get out there! Look at all the snow!"

A reluctant half-smirk curled my lips. He looked like a kid about to enter Disneyland for the first time. This was a day we all needed. Time to reconnect. Chill. We were each other's only real family, for one reason or another. Not everyone had shared. I hadn't shared. Simone hadn't shared.

It was time to pull out the stops. I was going to demand everything from her.

Simone laughed, a throaty sound that warmed me from the inside. Appreciating Connor's spontaneous affection, she hugged his forearms to her chest, giving them a warm squeeze before letting him withdraw them and turning to gaze at him over the edge of her seat. "You're so excited. I didn't know how much you loved skiing."

"He loves Christmas," Seth corrected from the seat behind me, reaching out and combing his fingers through Connor's shaggy blond hair in an affectionate caress. "All things holiday, including the twinkling lights, decorated trees, and most importantly, the TV specials."

"Special holiday Christmas movies are my jam," Connor agreed, his eyes dancing. In a more serious tone, he added, "Don't you find that somehow people are just better during the holidays? It's like they have the time to realize a capacity for kindness that they forget they have the rest of the year."

"Sure. Maybe," Simone shrugged, but her smile faded. For a few beats, her eyes took on a mile-long stare out toward the crowd of people milling around the chairlifts in the distance, clearly her mind taking her to another time and place. It was that same flash of something reflected in their blue depths that I'd seen earlier—that haunted look. If I had to guess, she didn't agree with Connor. Whatever secrets she had caused emotional injury.

We were all orphaned in some way, or we wouldn't have come together so easily and readily. I knew that we all had family stories of rejection, but Simone had never talked about her own other than to say she didn't go home anymore.

There were layers to uncover.

Mysteries to solve.

Pains to soothe.

I wanted to take that look from her eyes.

Cat and Beck pulled up next to my SUV in a truck that looked like it had seen better days. Mud splatter, now iced on from the cold of the overnight temperatures, covered its sides.

"You need to wash this thing," Seth called to Cat once we'd piled out into the crisp air, our feet sinking into thick snow with each step. He was the first to grab what he and Connor needed from the tail end as Cat hopped down from her own passenger side. Beck's vehicle had died somewhere north of the Sierras in his rush to drive in from Colorado the day before. He'd had to get a ride from his sister the rest of the way so he could finally corner Cat and have it out with her.

"No time," Cat grinned, lean and fit in her skiwear, her auburn hair mostly hidden under a black beanie. She'd driven from the wilds of Wyoming where she'd been hiding out, also arriving just the day before.

"She isn't going to have time for a while," her fiancé, Beck came around from the driver's side and enveloped her with his muscled form like a big man-cape. Her pale skin flushed a bright red color.

"Beck—" she protested, still new to the whole couple thing, but her smile never wavered, and when she looked at me, she mouthed the words "thank you", which was not what she'd said when I first told her Beck had shown up.

I winked.

Simone went to grab her boots and jacket from the back end of my SUV, and my eyes immediately appreciated the outline of the cleft of her ass. She looked like quite the ski bunny with her sleek white pants showcasing how long and shapely her legs were. Her full breasts, nipples hard in the cold air, were cupped by a fitted thermal, and I knew she was about to cover up those babies with a sweater and thick jacket. So pretty in transparent-when-wet lace. So hot when smashed against my chest in the hot tub. Sexy as fuck.

Leaning up behind her, ostensibly to grab my own boots and jacket, my own frame hulked out around her slight one. I let her feel my cock that was always semi-hard around her now. I know she felt it when I caught the barely perceptible intake of air.

"Your panties are in my pocket," I murmured in her ear.

"You like how they smell?" She sounded breathless.

"So fucking good." The last two words were a more of a harsh rasp.

Her breath stuttered out with soft puffs. Then she

whispered back, "My pussy is getting so wet."

I bit her ear, causing her to shiver. "I'll take care of her soon."

Breath a little shaky, Simone gave me a heavy-lidded side-eye over her shoulder and rubbed her ass against my rod just the slightest bit, giving my cock a thrill. I bit back a groan, my hips flexing against her softness under the guise of needing to reach farther back into the well of the car, and witnessed her lips open on another quick breath, before stepping back with my gear in hand.

Her face was flushed.

The pulse in her neck fluttered rapidly.

I refused to look away even when she quickly backed up several steps with her cumbersome gear to make room for Seth and Connor to get the rest of their gear, and tried to pretend nothing had happened, but she couldn't look away any more than I could. She zipped up her matching, fur-trimmed, white jacket. Her eyes stayed with mine until she was forced to kneel to buckle her ski boots.

My attention kept her hyperaware of me. That's what I wanted. Her focus on me. On our game. On what I might do to her. What she didn't know was that I was playing for keeps.

"Is everybody ready?" Connor asked while doing his heel-toe ski-boot strut backwards, trying to get us all moving. "C'mon!"

"We're coming," Cat called, shuffling awkwardly while trying to grab hold of her skis and poles. Beck grabbed them from her, somehow managing to hold both his and her gear. He bent to steal a kiss before they followed Seth and Connor.

Shooting a quick glance at Simone, I could see she was clearly a pro. As I closed the back end of the car and clicked the lock button on my key fob, she strolled confidently behind the rest of the group. When no one was looking, she glanced back at me over her shoulder with a playful wink and blew me a kiss.

Beautifully shaped. Plump. Natural artistry. I'd feasted on them last night. They were perfect. I managed to catch up in a few quick strides and cup her ass. My middle finger may or may not have traced the seam of her pants to the hot spot between her legs, giving the area a quick reminder rub.

Her head whipped around, her lips forming a silent, gasping "O" while her eyes canvased the parking lot for witnesses. No one was paying us any attention.

"Mr. Merrick, you're being rather forward. What kind of girl do you think I am?" she half-whispered with a look of mock affront. Of course, the twinkle in her eye negated the pretend shock. Then there was that hint of a breathless quality to her voice that told me she liked what I was doing.

"I think you're a tease, Ms. Marchand," I murmured, giving her ass one more gentle squeeze. "A girl who acts like a cock tease might get treated some kind of way."

"You're the one who left a girl hanging this morning." She pouted for effect. "I'd never do that to you." Have I said she is fucking adorable? I couldn't stop the grin from stretching across my face, her eyes warming as she took it in. It was a foreign feeling to be so light-hearted, but one I welcomed.

"Been thinking about that, have you?"

"You made promises," she replied with a pointed look before darting her eyes around again, looking to see if anyone could overhear our conversation. There was enough ambient noise between the Christmas music and the clomping of our boots through the icy parking lot that no one could hear what we said. We were in an intimate bubble that didn't allow room for others.

"Promises I intend to keep, but you have to earn them, Lips."

"Lips?" Her brows arched in question.

"For some reason, I keep picturing them." Beautiful. Full. Soft. I wanted to sink into them again.

"Any particularly place?"

"My fondest imagining is seeing them wrapped

around my dick."

"That can be arranged." She pursed her lips before adding, "But that's something *you* have to earn."

"Is that right?"

"I'll have to rate your efforts today."

"Orgasms?"

"Yup." She grinned big.

"Then we both better stay focused."

"Agreed."

Today was going to be a new day.

Garlands with decorative red bows and bright lights hung on anything that could stand still. The lodge was strung with them, lamp posts, and even some of the shuttle busses glowed with a few strands around wreathes mounted on the front grilles. All around us, there was a general air of merriment with joking, energetic conversations, and good-spirited razzing. Families, friends, couples were relaxed, smiling, mingling, laughing amid the backdrop of holiday rock music coming from speakers outside the lodge.

Many had grouped around the ski lift, queuing up to get a ride to the top of the first slope. From there, other lifts took the more skilled skiers clear up to the top of the mountain where the black diamond runs lay shrouded in clouds that were dumping fresh powder in the hills. The promised storm had begun delivering. Fat snowflakes fell from the sky like confetti, drifting on the air around us.

"This is my jam," Simone grinned, looking up at the top and closing her eyes on a deep inhalation of air. "I love the mountains. Fresh, crisp air. Speed. Riding the edge of fear and exhilaration. I used to live for the slopes when I was in high school."

"You haven't gone skiing much since?"

"Not so much. Life is busy. Once a year?" She shrugged, the joy on her face dimming as though she'd gone back to an unpleasant memory. The rest of our group had stopped near the other revelers and were snapping into gear, securing gloves and goggles. I looked back at her, wanting to see her smile again.

"Once I took a job at a resort. Taught beginners."

"You took a job?" She smirked. "I thought you were the original Richie Rich."

"Richie Rich?" I mirrored her expression and shook my head. "There's family wealth that is managed, I suppose."

"A legacy kind of upbringing?" she questioned. "And still you took on a menial job. Interesting."

It was my turn to grow introspective. "I had my reasons."

We stared at each other for a beat. She was waiting for me to elaborate, but now wasn't the time or place. With a nod of acceptance, recognizing that I wasn't going to give up secrets any more than she was just yet, she clicked into her skis.

I did the same, and we both pushed closer into our group.

"I've only done this once before." Cat laughed as she kept losing her balance and doing sudden windmills with her arms. She'd just put her skis on and, out of nowhere, simply fell over like a tree cut in a forest. *Timber* would have been an appropriate shout out to those around her.

"Cat!" Simone gasped.

"I'm all right." Cat laughed as she said this from the snow-packed ground, scrambling to try and get back up.

"You're like dead weight," Connor sputtered, almost landing on top of her when he tried to pull her up to her feet, only to have her fall back on her ass again. She laughed harder, not even trying to get up this time.

"You guys might want to go ahead," Beck chuckled, positioning himself so he could hook his hands under her arms and haul her back up to her feet. "We're going to need to go over some basics."

"We can all help with that," Simone offered.

"No way. I'm not willing to hold anyone else

back. Especially you. Weren't you supposed to go to the Olympics or some such thing?" Cat arched a brow, still clinging to Beck since her feet refused to remain under her.

"Is that right?" I looked down at Simone with an eyebrow arched, marveling at the new information. An Olympic athlete needed self-discipline. Hard work. Somehow, I wasn't surprised. Wasn't she working through her doctorate? There hadn't been a time I'd known her that she wasn't working her ass off toward a goal.

"Olympics?" Connor whistled appreciatively, nodding his head. "You must be really good."

"Yeah. Long ago. Didn't get the chance to try out," she said dismissively. The genuine smile she'd worn just a minute ago had morphed into the fake one that didn't touch her eyes. I wondered what had happened.

"Well, I still need to take it easy. I'm getting to be an old man," Seth offered, sending a dubious look up at the snowy hill. "I want to stay on the beginner slopes. Can't afford to break anything."

"How 'bout this." Conner moved in closer to let a family get past our group. We were effectively blocking easy access to the chair lift. "Let's pair off and do our own thing for the first part of the day to warm up. Then we can meet for lunch and play together the second half."

"Sounds perfect," Cat nodded.

"Noon. Main lodge," Connor offered.

Everyone agreed.

While Cat and Beck continued to fight a losing battle with gravity, since Cat couldn't keep her feet under her, I followed Simone. Easily, as though in sync, we glided around the chaotic family groupings still gearing up. It probably helped that my eyes were trained on her nicely rounded ass that was perfectly outlined by her tight ski pants. Every smooth shift of her hips and legs was easy to follow.

We joined the line to find it moving steadily, and in a few short minutes, the ski lift swept us into the air, carrying us up toward the top of the tree line.

"Your ass is perfect. I just thought I should tell you. It will avoid any confusion if you catch me staring at it at any point during the rest of the day."

She barked a short laugh. "All right. Same back."

"You like my ass?"

"I do. It looks grabbable."

"Oh, it is," I assured her.

She laughed again, and the musical sound was suddenly my favorite thing to hear.

"Feel free to test that out at any point today."

Her smile drifted away by degrees, and I knew

she was about to start pulling back. "Is this really a good idea? Us playing like this?"

"Why wouldn't it be?"

"I don't want to ruin our friendship." She looked down at the ski poles she held. "I've managed to fuck up every important relationship in my life until now. It just seems like we're about to jump into the deep end."

"Then we'll just have to swim."

"Topher—"

"From the first moment we met, I was interested."

Her eyes snapped to mine, a hint of surprise widening them. "You weren't."

"I was, but you were dating some guy." I shrugged, pushed away the aggravating memories of seeing her with someone else—someone who'd had the right to touch her in ways I wanted to.

She squinted into her memories before nodding. "Jason. I remember."

"And then you were done with him and met someone else. You dated three or four other guys in the last few years. I didn't think I was your type."

"See?" Her cheeks flushed a deep pink. It was like she was ashamed. "You're proving my point."

Confused, I asked, "What point is that?"

"I don't make good choices."

"Why weren't they good choices?" I mean, I agreed with her, but only because I knew I was the best choice, the last choice she needed to make if I got my way.

"Because I couldn't stick with them. After a few months, sometimes less, it was like I just couldn't waste anymore of my time with them. It's always like that. Every guy."

"That just means you learned what doesn't work for you."

"What if you don't work for me either?" The fear shimmered in her eyes, drawing her brows together with worry.

"That's life, but I don't think that's going to happen with us."

"That's just not acceptable, Topher. I need you in my life. You're important to me, and I can't let a time come when we can't be in the same space."

"Then we don't let that happen. We both actively work to make sure it doesn't happen."

"But—"

"I think you're worrying too much and not playing enough. Simone, truth or dare?"

She took a deep breath and released it, a crooked half smile that gave her a rueful expression. "I do overthink things. We're both adults. We can keep things simple. All right. Dare."

"Tell me a sexual fantasy."

"I…" She blinked at me, instantly flushed and simultaneously wary. She was afraid of telling me. Afraid of letting me inside where she was most vulnerable. Most private. Most secretive. "You'll think I'm a freak. I don't want to change how you think of me."

"Why don't I go first," I offered. "My fantasy is to tie you up so that you're completely helpless. Your body becomes my personal playground, and I make you come a few times with my mouth, my fingers, maybe a toy or two in your pussy and in your ass. Have you ever had ass play?"

She took a shaky breath and admitted, quietly, "No, but I want to."

"We can make it happen."

"Okay."

"So, after making you come over and over, I make you come again on my cock, and there's nothing you can do but take it."

Simone's eyes had dilated, gone half-mast with arousal, her lips parted as her breathing grew heavier. She liked what she was hearing.

"That story you told last night?" I added, continuing after she gave a short couple of nods, "Well, a new fantasy is to see you enact that for me. I want to watch you finger yourself until you come in front of me. I've had a permanent hard-on for that since you shared. In fact, thinking about that got me off last night."

"I can do that," she breathed.

The top of the mountain was coming into view. We'd be getting off in just a few minutes. I figured on waiting until we were on our next lift to see if she would respond, so it was a complete surprise when she leaned close, the warmth of her breath kissing my ear. Where it touched, the cold skin burned with heat.

She murmured, "I fantasize about public orgasms that are deliciously filthy and leave me feeling desperate for more. I think about being stuffed full of a hard, thrusting cock whenever and wherever the need arises because my lover can't wait another second to be inside me." Then she nipped my lobe before pulling back to gauge my reaction.

A charge of heat flashed down my spine straight to my dick, right when her words registered. Even surrounded by frigid temperatures, my cock grew thick and hard in an instant. I couldn't look away from her sultry eyes. She'd brought me under her spell with words alone.

Holy fuck.

Then we were forced off the lift, and I had to shove off the metal seat or else end up on the return trip back down the mountain.

Simone was already slicing through the powder ahead of me.

Chapter 4
Simone

Topher wanted to tie me up and fuck me full of orgasms.

He spoke my language. Did he know about me already? Mild alarm discomfited me until I realized how ridiculous I was being. There was no way. No one in the group knew.

But the imagery... Fuck me full of orgasms. The strong silent type, but with kinks. There was depth in still waters. I would just have to take it. Be at his mercy. And his goal was to make me come.

The image his words created in my fertile mind set off a chain reaction of instant raw lust. I could see myself at his mercy, letting him do exactly what he described. Heat poured through my veins, a gush of wetness dampening the crotch of my leggings. I felt it. I practically orgasmed from his words alone.

My heart danced a jig inside my chest, and fluttery tingles tickled the inside of my belly with the confession I'd whispered back. Excitement, and a little bit of fear of the forbidden, sent a burst of energy flooding through my body.

A cool down was needed.

I shoved ahead with my ski poles and hit the afterburners, racing ahead of Topher down the steep mogul run. Being that it was one of the harder runs, it was virtually empty. I knew he would chase me, and I realized this was foreplay.

It might have been a while since I'd gone down a course, but one did not simply forget years of training. This particular run was one I'd done countless times in another life. It was as natural as breathing for my legs to act spring-loaded, absorbing the movement around each snow obstacle, leaning into the angles effortlessly.

But it turned out I wasn't as fast as I used to be.

The wind whistled past my ears, freezing my exposed cheeks and lips as the thrill of the speed, and the anticipation of eventually being caught, kept me in suspense.

Risking a quick glance up over my shoulder on one turn let me see that Topher was fast catching up. Riding low, his muscular thighs flexed as he circumvented each mound of snow. Damn, he had good form. He looked as hot as ever… And that's when my ski caught an edge. In overcompensating, my skis skidded out from under me, popping off my feet as I spun around full circle in a snow angel position on my back. Less than a second later, Topher was crouched over me. I was still laughing at my goof, staring up at the snowflakes coming down.

"You all right, Lips?" he asked, smiling, sinking down beside me, but turning sideways to accommodate his skis.

"Peachy," I answered.

"You sure?"

"Maybe you should check."

"Maybe I should." He ran a hand down my arm, slid it over to my hip, and moved up under my jacket to cup my breast. His thumb zeroed in on my nipple through my sweater, swiping over it again and again, his eyes never leaving mine.

"Fuck…" I whispered, the magic already working. Building heat had me breathing heavier when I gasped out his name, "Topher…"

"It's important to be thorough," he murmured, and his hand slid down my ribcage to between my legs, where he cupped me like he owned me, squeezing before letting his thumb rub lazily a few more times over the layers of pants. So good and so frustrating all at the same time. Too many layers.

"That feels so…"

"I think you're going to be all right," he interrupted, his smirk evil. With a quick kiss on my nose, he shoved up onto his feet again and headed downhill with a quick salute my direction.

Really? Two could play that game.

There was a smaller lift down this back side of the mountain that went up to another part of the peak, which was where Topher was heading. I could see it in the distance. By the time I'd grabbed up my skis, clicked them back on and begun heading down again, he was more than halfway down the run. He was waiting by the smaller lift by the time I caught up.

Deliberately running into him.

"Oh, excuse me," I sing-songed, letting my skis get caught up with his, letting my body rub on his, letting my hand run around his waist under his jacket, down his abdomen to "catch" myself when, really, I used the opportunity to cup his hardened cock, doing a little rubbing and tugging through his pants while using my ski to unclip his ski from his boot when he didn't realize it because his eyes were about to roll back in his head.

Just as he muttered a heat-induced curse, I shoved off and propelled myself up toward the lift. Catching the first lift, I looked back over my shoulder to see Topher struggling to snap back into his skis, his eyes focused on me with a determined glint.

It was on.

Once I got off at the top, I took off down the front of the mountain face, dodging smaller groups and weaving around single skiers who clogged up the run. Topher caught up when I got cut off by a novice and had to slow or mow them down. He shot past me and changed course, steering toward the obstacle course of various sized jumps. When he slid out off a particular jump, I shot past him to trick off a snowbank or two. Before long, we were at the bottom of the hill grinning like fools, muscles shaky.

It was a game of frisk and release, kiss and run, one hour sliding into two while we covered as much of the mountain as we could. Before long, we were right back where we started. It was like we were a unit. Being with him, talking with him, our playfulness, was addicting. We'd never spent this much time alone, just the two of us.

I didn't want anyone else there.

It was strange. New to me. But I had to be careful. Topher was a good guy, and he deserved only the best. Some of the good feelings dimmed as I thought of that. It was going to be all right. I just had to remember this was strictly for fun. We'd both agreed to that.

"No one else is here yet," he said with a quick scan of the crowd.

"We're a little early—" I eyed the quaint lodge

in front of us. "—but if we go back up to the top again, we'll likely be late. We can go in and grab some drinks while we wait."

"Let's go in." He ran his hand over my backside on his way to the ski rack, a wicked glint in his eye as he slid past me. Even that one touch gave me goosebumps.

After securing our skis and poles to the metal rack outside the lodge, we went through the double doors into the warm ambiance of the restaurant, where the sound of families and soft rock filled the air. With families taking up all the tables in the restaurant, it was an easy enough decision to head into the more secluded bar area down the hall. Still, there was standing room only.

The reason why was immediately clear: several large-screen TVs around the bar displayed a football game.

At the far corner of the bar, pushed up against the wall, was space for a single person. Before it was taken by someone else, I grabbed Topher's hand and weaved through the tables. There wasn't a barstool, but I was sure we wouldn't be there long. He leaned into me, and I made sure to rub my ass back and forth—casually, of course—against his cock. I could already feel his cock pressing up against me insistently. He pushed back against me, his lips brushing against my ear.

"What would you like?"

"From the menu?" I arched a brow over my shoulder at him.

He grinned, but his look was heated. "For now."

"Pale ale."

Even after getting the bartender's attention and ordering, he didn't move away. Just pulled a bill from his pocket and set it on the table in front of me. Then, with his lips by my ear, he started working his magic again.

"Let's get back to the problem you started for me on the slopes," he murmured. "I could fucking pound nails with my dick the way you left me. There was no way to hide it."

"You started it," I laughed, and deliberately pushed my hips back again to rub on the steel length of him some more. He growled a moan in my ear with a muttered "fuck" that was more a puff of air.

Just imagining that length stretching me was getting me going. And if I was going to go that far, I wanted to go farther. I could imagine my teeth clenched to keep from snapping with each thrust as he pounded into me, bracing myself to keep from losing what would be the most deliciously hot feel of him moving inside me.

His hands went to my hips, but he didn't stop my movements. Instead, his fingers eased under the hem of my sweater, his actions hidden by my thick jacket. His rough fingers edged up my ribcage, pushed the wire barrier of my bra out of the way, and captured my breasts in his large hands.

Pure heat streaked south, adding to the ache between my thighs. I gasped and looked around the room. It was loud and busy, and no one was taking their attention away from the game. Its volume nearly overwhelmed the room between the audio of screaming fans from the actual game coming through the speakers and those around the bar, all talking, alternately shouting out advice to the screen and groaning with the team's actions.

No one knew that I was on the verge of panting out a moan as Topher's fingers rolled my nipples, alternating between rough play and gentle caresses. He'd tilted his head up toward the large screen as though involved in the game, but then he bent toward my ear again.

"Do you know what happens to little girls who play cock-tease?"

"What is that?"

"They get their first orgasm of the day."

He said it at the same time he squeezed both of my nipples particularly sharply before rubbing a gentle caress over them. I sucked in a gasp and closed my eyes as swirls of pleasure made their way to my clit, making it swell, creating a demand I couldn't ignore.

My pussy had been in a state of arousal for

hours, pulsing pleasurably with every teasing word, every playful touch. If he didn't finish me off, I was going to have to take matters into my own hands—as anticlimactic as that would be. I felt so needy. I wanted to come desperately, but it was more than that. I really wanted him to make me come.

I was almost disappointed when his hands left my breasts, until I realized one of them was heading south, sliding under the waistband of my snow pants. Was he following my fantasy? Oh shit. The shock of it—in the middle of a crowd—both tantalized and frightened me. My first reaction was to move to pull away, but then I stopped. Looked around. No one was watching me, but if they did happen to look, they wouldn't be able to tell that his hand was in my pants, working its way under the material of leggings. My clothing was bulky, and the bar top hid what he was doing.

And still, I held my breath.

His middle finger had just reached my folds, parted them in order to uncover my swollen clit, when the bartender returned with our drinks. I was on the verge of coming unraveled as I made eye contact with him. Topher's finger made a slow, light circle around the puffy bundle of nerves. My body felt shaky.

"Thanks," Topher nodded, and that's when I realized his free hand was accepting the drinks we'd ordered. "Give him the money, Lips."

His finger became more insistent. Rubbing.

Pinching. Plucking. He played with my clit, dipped into my pussy for the juices that seeped from me. My thoughts scattered.

"M-money?" I asked, looking down.

"You need to pay him," he whispered.

"Oh…" I spotted the bill he'd placed there earlier. Picking it up, I started to hand it over to the bartender at the same time as Topher's finger found its way inside. Fighting to keep my voice sounding even and not breathless, I said, "Thanks. No change."

Nodding, the bartender took the bill and hurried off. That's when Topher whispered, "Hold on to your beer, Lips. You're about to get a ride. Spread your legs."

I casually slid a foot sideways, and he slid his finger out and in, swirling and rubbing, pumping in and out. Then he spread my wetness back over my clit, circling it, pinching it, and I couldn't help the sharp, shallow breaths that puffed out from between my lips. It was when he wedged a second finger inside me that I moaned out loud, but luckily something exciting happened on the big screens around the room that had everyone cheering and shouting.

"Shhh," Topher whispered, working his fingers in and out of me while his thumb trailed over my clit. So close. I was so close.

"Topher…"

"I know."

"Please."

"Hold on."

Intimate whispers. Hushed. Desperate.

His fingers moved deeper, his thumb pressed and rubbed harder, and the magic sprang up from my toes, curling them in my boots before zinging up through all my nerve endings. When the pleasure hit, I nearly cried out.

"Shhhh…" Topher warned, his fingers still gently rubbing circles over the contracting folds.

My eyes closed, and my head fell back against his shoulder. For a few seconds, my legs felt like they going to give out. A few small contractions had me gripping the edge of the bar, but the magic chemicals circulating my body kept a lazy smile on my face.

That was amazing.

"You're so fucking hot, Lips," he whispered in my ear. He pulled his hand out of my pants, but I caught it, and gave the tip of his middle finger, still damp with my juices, a quick kiss, letting my own tongue slide out to taste myself on him.

"And you've been a good boy." I grinned back at him. "You'll be rewarded soon."

"You're going to be the death of me," he muttered, his large cock pressed against my ass. "You created a monster in my pants."

"Soon." I gave a short laugh at his growl, but I was definitely going to take care of him.

Facing forward again, ostensibly to watch more of the game, I suddenly saw a ghost from Christmas past on the other side of the bar, and froze. He'd found me again, just like last year. He'd managed to figure out where I was and shown up like a freaking cancer.

Lucian Bisson.

Even knowing there was a possibility I would see him, because he knew I'd spend some part of the holiday on the slopes, the shock of it, of having my dirty past so close to my shiny present, made me panic. Had he gotten the information out of my half-sister? She was the only family left I still spoke to. She would never knowingly give him information; I was sure of that.

"What's wrong?" Topher asked, likely having felt my body stiffen. His arms surrounded me in a warm, protective hug, his face resting against the hollow at the side of my neck. I wanted nothing more than to savor it, cocoon myself against the reality bearing down on me, but I wanted to shield this part of my life from him. From everyone who mattered.

"N-nothing." I turned to face him, relaxing my

facial muscles into a sensual smile. "I was just wondering if any of the others were here. I wouldn't want them to wait. Would you check while I readjust in the bathroom?" I gestured with a quick nod toward the door near the exit.

"All right. We're not done yet," he warned, but his eyes assessed me, looked to see if there was more.

"We've got all day." I hated that I was trying to make him leave after the sexiest orgasm I'd ever had by someone else's hand, but I knew Lucian would be making his way toward me in seconds. It wasn't a confrontation I wanted to have with Topher present.

"I'll be right back."

As soon as he'd gone, I walked toward the bathroom where it was quieter, near the exit, less crowded. Within seconds, Lucian was there.

"Simone Marchand. Beautiful as always." Lucian's soft voice still had the power to make my skin crawl. I fought the cringe that wanted to take hold of my face as he stepped closer; on the verge of being too close. Memories of our last encounter swarmed. Ugh. They were ugly. I didn't want them tainting my time with Topher, and I had no idea what was going to come out of his mouth.

Lucian wasn't as tall nor as muscular as Topher because he didn't want to look like a barbaric ruffian. Lucian, coming from an illustrious family from within the elite circles of French society, cultivated a more slender, elegant image. He'd been ambitious, wanting to cushion his family coffers with my vineyard.

I'd crushed on him as a teenager when he first joined our family winery. He'd become the manager of operations when my dad was still overseeing the business. For years I'd watched Lucian with lovestruck eyes while he couldn't have been bothered to even acknowledge me. It hadn't deterred me.

I'd thought he was the epitome of gorgeous manhood, blond with a charming smile, until I'd learned otherwise. The charming smile always left his blue eyes hard and cold. Calculating. He was an opportunist. A user and an abuser. He'd developed a sudden interest in me when I turned twenty-one, much to my absolute delight.

He'd discovered that I'd inherited the winery.

I didn't find out until later.

"Lucian," I acknowledged evenly, squaring off. "What are you doing here?"

"Your sister told me you'd be here," he said, with what I was sure he considered a charming smile. In my eyes, it looked reptilian.

I cocked my head and narrowed my eyes, studied his face for a moment. How could I have ever thought he was attractive? I shook my head at my own naivete. "Come now, Lucian. She would never do that. She knows I want nothing to do with you."

His wince was for show, dimming his smile for a moment before it came back, bright, and shiny and fake. "Oh, Simone, I deserve that. An apology is long overdue."

"Yeah, whatever. So how did you actually find me?"

"It was your sister, but she was talking with your mother on the phone. I happened to be with your mother at the time, going over the financials." He shrugged and gave me his signature smile, let his eyes roam the area. "This was a special place for us, no? When I met with your father?"

"No. It was a special place for me with my dad. You were incidental."

"We had intimate time here. I remember every detail." He let his eyes drift over my body. "You snuck into my suite. We made love. It should have been the beginning of our partnership. My behavior in the past was foolish, and I have wanted to make amends since then."

"Fine. I accept your apology. You could have sent a card. My sister would make sure I received it."

"But then I wouldn't see you. I couldn't help myself. I've missed you."

He missed the idea of owning the vineyard. That

was what he missed. What was going through his head? Did he actually think I was so weak-willed that I would believe the bullshit he spewed? My anger was on slow simmer. "So you came looking for me. How romantic."

"You know that I still care about you."

"Do I?" The laugh was spontaneous, if lacking in actual humor. It was more a remark on the irony of his statement.

"I won't tell you a silly story of love. It would be a lie, and you wouldn't believe it besides. No, people like you and me, we don't have the capacity for love, but we can build partnerships. Successful partnerships. I don't love you, but you know I respect you." He tilted his head with a smile that would have melted my heart when I was eighteen. It did nothing for me now.

"I seem to have lost that knowledge in the last two years. Look, don't waste my time. Cut through the bullshit, Lucian. Why are you actually here? What do you want?"

"To make amends. I've wanted to for quite some time." He reached out to touch the hair on my shoulder, but I stepped just out of reach. He gave me a sad smile, but I could see it was practiced. "It takes two people working together to succeed in a relationship, and I realized soon after you left that I might have overreacted. My actions were harsh. I should have been more understanding of your…needs."

Remembered shame from long ago blossomed anew. His look of horror. Disdain. Disgust. The heat from the slap he'd delivered burned fresh across my face as though it had happened three seconds ago rather than almost three years ago.

"Go fuck yourself, Lucian. Don't contact me anymore. I won't bother telling you again. There will never be anything between us. If you don't leave me alone, you'll be sorry. I promise."

"What can you do to me?" he smirked. "You need me." He reached a hand out to grasp a curl on my shoulder. I slapped his arm away, which only made him grin wider. "I've touched more than this in the past. Don't you remember?"

I pointed a finger up into his face, and snarled, with satisfaction, "I let you stay on despite what you did to me, but my patience is running out. You will back off or I will fire your ass. You own a few shares in the company, but they are contingent on you remaining with the company."

It was the first time I'd stood up to him, and it made him pause, had him looking deeper into my eyes. When he realized I meant what I said, that I was meeting his look without flinching, his expression twisted with sudden rage.

"You can't fire me," he sneered, his hand snaking out to grab my hair in a tight fist, holding me immobile. "You need my expertise."

"Go ahead. Test me." I gave him a triumphant

smile. "That's what you can tell yourself on your way out the door."

"Listen, bitch—" He was suddenly slammed up against the wall, a muscular arm pinned across his throat. Muscles tense.

"Call her a bitch one more time, and I will become your living nightmare," Topher growled, inches from Lucian's wide-eyed surprise. The deadly glare he skewered Lucian with promised a beat-down. Begged for it.

Tendrils of warmth unfurled around my heart. Topher was protecting me. He was going all caveman. It was a side I hadn't seen before. I'd seen the kindness, the brilliance, the patience, the loyalty, and the hotness. But I hadn't seen this. So many facets. Complexity. He was even more than I had realized.

"What's the problem here?" he asked me, a brief chin motion my direction, his tone just barely controlled, while menacing Lucian with a deadly glare. When I didn't answer quickly enough, he asked Lucian, "Who are you?"

"Simone's fiancé." Lucian suddenly grinned at seeing the new murderous look in Topher's eyes, even while clinging to the powerful forearm that threatened his windpipe. He'd recovered enough to talk but didn't realize he was poking the lion. "Are you the one she's playing with now? None of you ever last. Eventually, she'll come back home because she belongs to her own kind."

"Ex-fiancé," I growled with a shudder. "I will never get over what you did to me. Do yourself a favor and hear that."

"What did he do to you?" Topher's jaw was clenched, nostrils flared. All it would take was a word from me, and Lucian would be toast.

Lucian must have realized that because, after a quick assessment of the situation, he held up a hand. "Let me go."

"Just let him go," I repeated. "I don't want to cause more of a scene here."

Topher turned his attention on me, then, reluctantly, backed off a step. It was enough for Lucian to give a final sneer and slink away, but Topher wasn't done with me yet. When he spoke, his tone was harsh. "Tell me."

The protective anger in his eyes was addicting. Arousing. No one had ever stood up for me before, but neither did I want to have to bail Topher out of jail. "If I tell you, you'll want to go after him. I don't need you to do that."

"Simone—"

"Later." I grasped hold of his jacket and pulled him in for a nip on his bottom lip. He groaned, so I did it again, lingering to soothe the sting I'd created, until he was taking over the kiss, angling my head to deepen it until we were both panting again.

"You are making me crazy," he snarled into my

mouth, a sharp edge to his dark expression. "He touched you, and I didn't get to kick his ass."

"He's gone."

"But you're mine."

Then he pulled me toward the bathroom. The door led to a single stall, and he pulled me in, shut the door and locked it before spinning me to face the sink. The entire wall was mirrored.

"Topher…"

"Stop me now if you don't want this," he said, a fierce determination in his eyes. He was unzipping my jacket, spreading it wide, and pulling up my sweater. With my bra still shoved awkwardly away from my breasts, they were on display. Full. Nipples pebbled.

"Oh, God," I whispered when his hands cupped my breasts and his thumbs and forefingers pinched my already-stiff nipples hard, rubbing on them, wiping out the taint of my past with the pleasure of the now. "Yes."

I could see everything he was doing in the mirrors. There was nothing in my memories to rival the heat of this moment, the pleasure coursing through me. My hands reached back to find his erection, which hadn't gone down. If anything, it had grown thicker, longer, and harder. This was almost more than I could take.

"Fucking beautiful," he muttered roughly,

pinching my nipples and soothing them with gentle swirls in a way that showed he felt like he owned them. Then his hands were at my waist, popping the clasp, unzipping the fly, and shoving them down my hips along with my leggings.

"Topher…" I gasped, the image of his large form and big hands on my body as much a turn on as what he was doing. Slick wetness coated my pussy.

"Good girl," he murmured, while I quivered at his rough caress on my bare mound, overcome with lust so powerful it left me wobbly. I needed this. I needed him. His fingers moving through my wet folds, finding the empty place that needed to be filled.

I could hear the white noise of the crowd of people watching the game just beyond that door, and he was going to fuck me full of orgasms just feet away.

"Yes," I encouraged him, spreading my legs without shame. "Do it."

"Where does my dick go?" he whispered against my ear. "Put it where you think it belongs."

"Inside me," I whimpered, reaching back behind me to unsnap his pants and pull out his hot, thick length. "Do you have a condom?"

"Wallet."

I relished the hissing sound of air expelling from his teeth as I pumped his length while he fumbled with the zipper pocket on the side of his ski pants. Then he was rolling the condom into place, and I bent over the sink to put him right where I wanted him. In one move, he pushed his way deep inside me, stretching me to capacity with a delicious burn, and paused. Our eyes met in the mirror.

Mine were full of need. His looked tortured with pleasure. A muscle in his jaw twitched.

"Okay?" he managed to ask through clenched teeth. He was holding back. He didn't want to hurt me.

"No. I need you to move. Fuck me, Topher. Fuck me hard." My voice quavered with emotion.

"We're going to have to do this hard and fast. Hold on."

He didn't need any other command. Drawing back, his hand moved up my torso to grasp my breasts, then he pulled me upright and drove into me hard. Fast. Reaching behind me, I grabbed hold of his neck, desperate to hold on as I balanced on my tiptoes.

I could see his cock channeling into me in the mirror, each thrust of his hips making the pleasure sharper, hotter until I had trouble keeping my mewling quiet.

He pounded into me, filling me, stretching me to the point of feeling a burn through the pleasure, when one of his hands slid down to my throbbing, swollen clit, pinching and rubbing it hard. That's when I fractured. Came harder than I'd ever come before. Nervous system short-circuited. My body jerked. Convulsed against him, contracted around his still-thrusting cock.

My cry was cut off by Topher's other hand leaving my breast to cover my mouth. The orgasm went on and on as he kept pumping into me, plucking at my clit, his lips murmuring words in my ear that I couldn't make out until his own guttural shout was damped by his lips pressing into my neck. It was several moments before he lifted his head.

Breathing ragged, our eyes met in the mirror again. Both of us looking grave.

I felt exposed. Vulnerable. Then he turned his head, kissed my temple, and cupped my contracting folds in a primitive claim, deliberately running his fingers, wet with my own cum juices, up my torso to where my breasts quivered with each breath I took, and gave a gentle caress to each nipple, spreading my juices over them. My sensitized body quivered with a mini-contraction at the touch.

"It'll be my cum next time," he said firmly, a promise in his eyes. "You're beautiful, Simone. Your brilliance has always been my private torment because I thought I couldn't have you. And I'm not going to lie. Now that we've done this, I'm going to fight like hell to keep you."

He slid his fingers back to my pussy, gave it a

final caress, then bent to pull my leggings and pants back up. Turning me around, he sucked first one nipple, then the other, causing fresh mewling sounds of pleasure to escape my lips, before looking down at me again.

I still couldn't put words together. Did I even know what to say to that?

"You've been warned."

Chapter 5
Topher

"Food! I'm starving. All that exercise did me in. Fuck. I must be out of shape." Seth scowled at the thought, shrugged, then took a huge chomp of his burger.

"Such a caveman. For the record, I have no complaints about your shape." Connor grinned, picking up his own burger and licking a stray drop of ketchup from his finger before digging in.

Seth growled in response, then ruined the effect by wriggling his eyebrows suggestively, which made Connor give him a swoony look.

After locating the rest of our group, we'd found space large enough to fit all of us—scooting two tables of four together—and ordered food. It was pub food, and within a short time, the waitress had brought over trays of burgers and fries.

"You still haven't told us how your studies are going," Catrina called across the table as she dumped an absurd amount of ketchup on her plate. "Human sexuality. Sounds…sexy."

"Partly, it is," Simone winked.

Simone had put on her public face. She was smiling, talking in her usual carefree, quippy style, but now I could see past all that. There was a sadness in her eyes that she covered up with a playful façade, and it struck me that it had been there for as long as I'd known her. She mourned a loss, and I needed to know what…or who…that loss was.

Had she loved that asshole? The thought made me burn with jealousy. I'd heard part of their conversation, and the primitive male in me had risen up, needing to stake a claim. Beating Lucian's ass was my first thought, but not wanting to do time had chilled that impulse. Taking her against the sink in the bathroom, showing her and anyone who thought otherwise that she was mine, was the next urge, and one I couldn't deny. Every part of me wanted every part of her.

"Talk," Connor heckled her, picking a fry up off his plate and tossing it across the table at her. She grabbed it off her tray and ate it, a smirk tilting her lips. "What other cool sex shit do you get to study for your PhD?"

"Don't get me all hot and bothered here," Seth warned, his dark eyebrows coming together over the bridge of his nose while shooting a pointed look at Connor.

"Actually," Simone shook her head with a chuckle, "over the course of history, you'd be surprised at the different sexual practices that have been documented, practices that current standards of society—not to mention laws—consider degenerate or immoral. Did you know there was a book published back in the 17th century called *The School of Venus*, among other things, with racy conversations between young women and images of sex toys and positions? And, there was a funny bit from the turn of the 19th century. Women could be diagnosed with a condition called hysteria, which was described as being antsy, full of nerves, wound up, that kind of thing. And one of the treatments for that condition was to go to the doctor for a 'pelvic massage'." She delivered the air quotes around the words.

Her eyes twinkled as she looked around the table for everyone to put two and two together.

"Hold up," Beck grinned. "What you're saying is guys would send their wives to the doctor to get fingered?"

"Basically." Simone shrugged. She sipped her iced tea before continuing with a grin that stretched cheekily across her face, "The female orgasm was not a widely accepted fact until sometime in the mid-1900s. That's when Masters and Johnson researched and recorded this supposed rumored, mythical occurrence."

I smirked at her use of the word mythical, knowing that I had managed to get Simone off twice in the last twenty minutes or so. And I had plans for more. With that decided, I dug into my burger, suddenly ravenous.

"So, guys couldn't get their wives off, and their wives started getting pissed off?" Cat asked, appreciating her own cleverness if her grin was anything to go by. "Then the doctor would make a house call or something."

"Crazy, right?" Simone toyed with a fry on her plate as she spoke. "Anyway, I'm starting to think about my dissertation. I've been considering how culture has changed and will continue to change, maybe as it relates to family dynamics, and the ramifications of that change over time. I'm thinking about comparing the microcosm of different family settings with how the larger macrocosm in various societies handled, and handles, the evolution of women—you know, as we develop our sense of sexuality without it being defined by a patriarchal society. I've still got about a couple of years to develop it, you know, really flesh out my ideas and put together the sources I'm collecting before I can present my proposal for consideration. It's kind of a lot of work. Intimidating on my bad days."

"But then you will be Dr. Simone Marchand," Cat piped up. "So proud of you."

"Well, don't be too proud too soon. It will be a

while before I get through everything and defend my work by committee. I've heard a lot of people get hung up on the dissertation part."

"You won't," I said evenly, knowing it to be true. This woman knew what she wanted, and she was going to go for it.

"Yeah, well, that's the plan. Cross the finish line." She smiled cheerfully, but then her eyes slid over mine impersonally, and that's when I knew that the cost of our moment of vulnerability, the price I had to pay for catching a glimpse behind the curtain, was her pulling away emotionally. She was likely telling herself what a bad idea this had been. Us. What we'd done together.

No way I was going to let that happen. Setting my burger back on the plate, I wiped my hands and mouth with my napkin and set it back in my lap.

"So how did you all do on the slopes?" I asked, but casually moved my hand to her thigh. Our game was still on. No escape. It was only a split-second pause in bringing the fry to her lips, but it was enough for me to know I had her full attention.

"My ass hurts." Cat rolled her eyes, wiggling on the bench. "I kept landing on it. I thought snow was supposed to be soft."

"I'll rub it and make it better," Beck promised, but there was a definite gleam in his eyes.

"Are you still talking about her ass?" Seth arched

his brows.

"I could talk about her ass all day long," Beck smirked.

"Please don't." Cat shook her head and turned her attention to Simone. "How'd you guys make out?"

"Make out?" Simone suddenly choked on her spit, likely thinking of all the ways I'd violated her pussy since we'd gotten up this morning. I moved my hand up Simone's thigh as I leaned into the table to reach for my own drink with my free hand. She tensed. I waited to see if she would stop me. She didn't.

"We had a blast," I answered, letting my hand move up to that sweet spot between her thighs. "Didn't we?"

My thumb circled the right spot, and I knew this because her legs went lax and opened for me. She leaned into the table, covering the movement of my hand, and gave an enthusiastic nod.

Only I could hear the faint breathless quality to her voice when she said, "It's been so long since I skied. Ages, really. School's kept me busy for a few years now."

I pinched at her clit through the slippery material of her pants and underlayer of legging. It was going to feel both good and frustrating. Before long, she was going to be begging me to finish her off. I just had to be patient. It seemed to be the only way to break through her barriers.

"Maybe you'll come more often now that you remember how much fun it is. Don't you think? We should do this more often," I offered with an innocent smile. Meanwhile, her hips jerked against my hand, and I knew it was time to pull back. Later, I would make her fuck my fingers while she played with her own clit.

We were also going to talk. I gave a final pinch and rub before casually grabbing some of my own fries. And yes, there was a hint of her fragrance mixing with the scent of my fries, and it was heavenly. She watched me pop them into my mouth, watched me casually lick my two fingers that were just between her legs.

"Yeah," she inhaled. Her mouth had parted ever so slightly, watching me before she turned a bright smile on the others. "Those slopes have a lot of memories for me. They took me back to some good times."

There was no way I was going to be able to get her off here in front of everyone at the table without them knowing, but I wanted her thinking about me and not the asshole, Lucian. I wanted her to remember that I made her feel good. That I appreciated her. That we were very possible. And maybe I was discovering that I had a little bit of asshole in me because I was happy to leave her wanting. I could get her nice and hot and leave her that way for a while.

Simone bit her lip, wriggled her ass in her seat as though she were somewhat uncomfortable, but there was a new frustration in her expression, a barely caught side glance that showed me she didn't appreciate being left hanging. That was fine. I preferred her mad at me and wanting me than feeling alienated and alone. I rounded my eyes innocently and picked up my burger again.

"You should finish your burger." I gave Simone my best version of earnest encouragement. "You'll need your strength for later."

"Later?" Beck asked.

"She was kicking my ass on the slopes. I want a rematch."

"Just don't break anything. We have an amazing dinner planned for tonight, and a trip to the hospital is not in the cards," Connor warned.

"Better to risk it all on the jet fuel cocktail you made us last night?" Cat snarked. "That kicked my ass. And Simone's, I might add."

"It sure the hell did. You missed the kiss she laid on Topher after you guys left the hot tub last night," Seth chuckled, pushing his plate out of the way enough to lean his crossed forearms on the table.

"It was hot," Connor agreed, "and I'm only into dick, so that's saying something."

"My dick," Seth warned.

"Of course," Connor winked. "I'll show you how much I'm into your dick later."

"Wait, she kissed him? Really?" Cat looked at Simone. "You didn't say anything."

"It was just part of the game." Simone shrugged, but then she wiggled in her seat again. Relieving the ache I'd left her with?

Now Cat had a big grin. She turned it on Connor. "So, you're making more of this magic potion tonight?"

"Absolutely. I've come up with a name. We can call it Connor's Screaming Sex Machine."

"Subtle. I like it," Beck smirked.

"Well, Sex on the Beach is already taken, and besides, there's no beach here. Maybe we could call it Sex in the Snow?"

"Not so hot-sounding," Seth protested. "Sounds like you'd be getting important parts potentially frozen off."

"So, Connor's Sex Machine it is." Beck toasted with his soda. He drained it and set it back down, pushing his own plate out of the way.

"Screaming Sex Machine," Connor corrected. "That's a key word."

"Got it." Beck nodded, leaning back in his chair with a sigh. He had an arm around the back of Cat's chair. "You ready for more torture?"

"No. I'm not. I'm stuffed, and I don't want to go back up on the slope," Cat groaned, rubbing her belly. She leaned into Beck, looking ready to fall asleep on his shoulder, her eyes taking on the food coma-glazed look.

"We could go back to the pad and rest," Beck offered, rubbing his chin across the top of her beanie affectionately.

"And we need to get started on tonight's dinner," Seth offered up, looking to Connor for confirmation. "We could catch a ride with Cat and let the two lovebirds here play on the slopes more."

"Lovebirds?" Simone scoffed, shaking her head, but her eyes slid to mine quickly as though gauging my reaction.

"We'd appreciate that," I nodded, sliding a grin her way before adding, "…don't get up here much. We have some unfinished business."

"Unless you needed help," she asked politely, then squirmed in her seat again. Was that anticipation? Did she think I was going to finish her off at the table once everyone was gone?

"I have my beefcake helping me," Seth grinned, wrapping his arms around Connor. "Dinner will be ready by seven. Just make sure you're home by then."

"Will do." It was only when everyone else had left the table that my eyes and tone grew serious. "We need to talk."

"Talk, huh?" Her smile faded, to be replaced with a scowl. "So that was the plan. Get me all hot and bothered again, but just so you can get me to pour my heart out to you."

"I want to talk about what just happened." The lunch rush was fading. There were only a few families seated at tables, but none were near us.

"What if I don't feel like talking about this, Dr. Phil? Who do you think you are that you can insist on talking—"

"I'm your best friend and the guy who plans on giving you as many orgasms as you can take. That's who I am."

Her sigh was long and drawn out, giving her a few seconds to gather her words before she said, "We're just supposed to be having fun, right? I mean, we're not getting all serious or anything."

"I'm serious. I've always been serious about you."

"What does that mean?" Her eyes went wide.

She wasn't ready to hear my truth just yet, so I deflected. "Tell me why this guy still calls himself your fiancé. What's the story with the two of you?"

"See, that's a big story, and I don't know if I want to just throw it out on the table like it's normal lunchtime conversation. I mean, do you trust me?"

"Completely and absolutely." There was no hesitation in my answer.

"Really." That gave her pause. Her brows furrowed again. "Then tell me a story that sits in your soul like a cancer. Makes you doubt yourself on a regular basis."

"I walked in on my dad and one of my teachers having sex."

Her lips parted ever so slightly. She hadn't expected me to come through.

"Football practice was cancelled. Bad weather. Anyway, I was home unexpectedly early. Saw that my dad was home, which was strange, and another car was in the driveway. I went in thinking we had company, which would have been stranger still, since my mother was away in Chicago on a business trip." My eyes closed a moment as the old memory became clearer, traveled to the present from the past.

"Wow," she murmured in a softer response.

"They were in my parents' bedroom. The woman fucking my father was the new PE teacher at my high school. Young. Hot. All the guys wanted a piece of her, and she was freshly graduated. Only three or four years ahead of us. I could hear them.

They'd left the door open, so I caught them in profile. She was riding my dad, her tits perky and perfect, bouncing up and down. Then I caught my father's eyes. At once, I was both horrified and turned on." The heat of embarrassment warmed my neck as it always did. I had to clear my throat, look down at my nearly empty plate.

Simone's hand went to my leg, gave it a comforting squeeze. "That's a pretty fucked up situation. I'll give you that."

"What was fucked up was how I remembered her tits for years after, since I was only seventeen. Even more fucked up was how my mother attacked me for making my father tell her about the affair when she came home from her trip." It was the first time I'd felt alone. Alienated.

"She got mad at you?" Simone scowled, her expression turning fierce.

"Apparently, this was not news to her. She'd been aware the whole time, and it wasn't the first time. They'd both decided to pretend nothing was going on."

"What the actual fuck?"

"I didn't understand it at the time, but they'd worked out their relationship and were satisfied with it. Only when I was older did I realize my dad was a sexual being, and my mother wasn't at all." It was my first realization that life was far more complicated than I realized, and people had all different kinds of relationships.

"Yet, they stayed together?"

"No. It was too much that I knew. That fucked up the whole delicate balance they'd had. No one could pretend anymore. My mother never forgave me or my dad. She moved to Chicago when I was a freshman in college. Got a new job. She leaves me brief messages on my birthday. I still see my dad now and then, but it's so awkward, we both avoid it. On a regular basis, I wonder what life would have looked like if I'd just gone to my room, if I'd not gotten in the way of what they had going on. I know I should have minded my own business, but did they make it my business by not being more careful while I was still living in the house? I don't know."

"That's how you're an orphan in this group?"

"Yup." I turned to her. "Now it's your turn."

As she looked at me, likely trying to decide what to say, a dull flush worked over her cheeks. "This is stupid. Your story is not about how fucked up you are. It's about how other people's fucked-up decisions affected you. My story is strictly about how fucked up I am."

"So, tell me."

"Why? So you can be my shrink? Thanks, but no thanks."

"No. Tell me, because at the very least, I'm one of your best friends. Friends trust each other."

Her nostrils flared. Silence fell for a few eternal seconds before she took a deep, shaky breath and looked away. "I am a freak. I've been sexually charged since I was sixteen years old and first saw the new ski instructor at the Mountain Sky Ski Lodge up by Tahoe. He was hot. Barely twenty. And I wanted to eat him up. Then there was the guy, married, had a family, was kind of a silver fox, and I thought he was hot, too. Had "daddy" fantasies about him. Sex was almost all I could think about. Skiing and sex. Didn't give a shit about anything else."

"That's not strange. Sounds amazing."

"Yeah, well, it would be if I'd left it there, but I didn't. My dad died when I was eighteen, and that's when I lost it. Gave up on going to the Olympic trials to compete. He was my world. My rock. Then he was gone. At that point, I started engaging in dangerous behavior. My first serious sexual experience was in the mechanic's shed after the ski lifts were closed."

"The ski instructor?"

"No. He was gone by then, but I had let him finger me to orgasm."

"So, who was the guy in the mechanic's shed?"

"Someone I'd noticed earlier during my attempt to train. He'd been checking me out, so I knew he thought I was attractive. He was a good-looking guy, middle-aged, still fit, and I was ready to fuck. I didn't care. Part of the challenge was to see if I could get him to fuck me."

"And he did, of course."

"Bent me over the hood of a car and pounded me hard. I loved it, but it wasn't enough. We did it again the next day, middle of the day, and I caught one of the other assistants watching us. He and I made eye contact, and I could tell he was jacking off. Huge turn on. The day after that, I sucked him off while the mechanic fucked me for a final time. And I'm not ashamed of any of that."

"No reason you should be."

She frowned, studied my expression for authenticity, then continued. "Then there was this one time, after I found out my stepmother had decided I didn't need my ski gear anymore and gave it all away while I was in college, that I went to a bar. There was a frat party going on, and I convinced two of the guys to fuck me in the back alley. It was good. They were hot. And I wasn't ashamed of that either." There was no pleasure in her fake, shiny smile. It belied her words.

"So where does Lucian come in?"

"I'd had a crush on him from the time I was sixteen. He worked for my father at the family business. He'd been there a few years, run the day-to-day operations of the place. He was the only one who'd turned down my advances—until I turned twenty-one. That's when I received my shares in the company. Before that, they'd been in trust. Then he came on to me, and we started dating. Got engaged. I thought I was in love, and finally, we fucked. It was awful. He didn't do it for me, so I thought spicing things up would be good for us. I'd heard about an exclusive club down in L.A., and he agreed to come. He was horrified and called me a degenerate, which put me off. I told him he was incapable of making me come, so he slapped me. I ended the relationship and went on to fuck three guys in front of an audience that night. When I looked into the crowd, he was there, watching. I let him see me come over and over again. It was one of the hottest nights of my life."

I was silent for a moment, processing. She took that to mean that I was disgusted, and tears filled her eyes.

"So, you see, he still wants to own half the business, regardless of who I am, and now you know what a sick person I am because even though I'm not interested in random guys anymore, just remembering all of these experiences turns me on. I like the idea of being watched and watching. The thought of experimenting with toys and tools excites me. And that's why we can't ever be anything serious." She swept up out of her seat, swiped her jacket off the chair and practically ran from the room.

But she wasn't getting away that easily.

Judging from my own stiff cock, we were both

due another session.

Chapter 6
Simone

Shame warred with arousal.

My pussy was wet and throbbing with the memory of being fucked, my body expertly manipulated for maximum effect, while others looked on. It was almost as exciting now as it had been in that moment. There was no way this was ever going to be something anyone could understand. There was no way Topher would want to get involved with someone as fucked up as I was.

He caught up to me at the car, our skis and poles under one arm. I didn't want to see the look in his eyes—surely one of disgust, or at the very least, disappointment. Seeing that would be my undoing. I needed time. I needed to build up my shield again, the smile that showed the world everything was just fine.

I couldn't get there now.

Instead, I stood facing the passenger door, waiting for him to unlock it. He didn't. He dumped the skis by the back hatch, came around to my side of the car, and pushed up behind me, his hot breath by my ear. I shuddered, all my nerve endings feeling raw and exposed.

"We aren't done, Lips." He pushed his hips into mine and his hard cock found a home in the cleft between my legs. Involuntarily, I pushed back against it, craving the feel of him inside me again. There was a growl to his whispered words when he said, "That's it. Rub against me. See, while I don't want to see other guys fucking you now, your stories got me hot as fuck, so if you're sick, then so am I."

"It turned you on?" My breath hitched on the back of my emotions.

"You can feel me," he grunted, sliding his dick along my cleft again. "You want to know what else? I ran into my old PE teacher at the grocery store late one night a few years back, and you know what she did?"

"What?" I asked on a moan, sliding my ass against his dick.

"She gave me a blow job in my car. I finally got my hands on her tits."

"You did?" I gasped as a wave of heat pulsed

between my legs imagining it, along with a sharp spark of jealousy.

"I did," he growled, trailing his fingers up under my sweater again, finding my nipples and pinching at them roughly until I whimpered with need. "But you know what?"

"What?"

"They weren't near as perfect as yours."

"Topher—"

"Get in the car. I know a place."

"But I need—"

"I know what you need. Trust me."

It was less than a minute before we were in the car with the gear tossed haphazardly in the back. Wanting to drive him as crazy as he had driven me, my hand was in his lap, grasping the steel length of his cock. I wanted it inside me again and again. He was making me an addict. It was what I was afraid of and drawn to at the same time.

"We're almost there," he said, breathing heavily, his hand dropping to cover my own, making me squeeze his thick length as a soft, rumbling groan slipped from deep in his chest.

There was a lookout point away from the town on one of the back roads. It was there, amid the trees, that he took us. I unzipped him as he parked, pulled him out, and gazed at his perfect, hard cock, ready to swipe the precum off his tip with my tongue.

"I've wondered how you would taste," I murmured, letting my lips cover his crown, only.

"Fuck," he whispered reverently, watching from above.

He was undone, and I couldn't get enough of him. He bunched my hair out of my face, keeping it in his fist and controlling my movements. I could barely fit my lips around him, and the feel of his hands directing me had my own hand shoving between my legs to reach my pussy.

"Unbutton your pants," Topher commanded, and the moment I did, his own hand dove under my ski pants and leggings to slide between my slit folds, right where I wanted him. "I plan on putting my tongue there, Lips. I plan on fucking you with my tongue. What do you think of that?"

A warm gush of need flooded my pussy, making me whimper yet again, and he gave a faint chuckle.

"We'll have to do that soon. I want my mouth and cock all over you and in you, do you hear me?" He let his finger slide down farther until he was spreading my own juices over my puckered spot, past my pussy. I'd done a lot of things, but I hadn't done that before, and the thought of it had me moaning again.

"I need you," I whispered, pulling away from him.

"Pull your pants down. Sit in my lap and face the window." He said this while easing his seat back and digging another condom out of his wallet.

Then I was sitting on him, and I immediately felt him at my opening, sliding so deep inside me I knew I would always feel him there. He pulled my sweater back up, roughly shoving my bra out of place again so he could get to my tits. With his fingers rolling my nipples, I couldn't sit still. Bracing my hands on his spread thighs, I took him as far as I could, gasping as I rode his thick, hard cock. I'd been turned on for so long, this was a close thing. All sensation was concentrated on the heat growing exponentially between my legs.

"So close," I hissed.

"Come on my cock. I want to feel you."

Looking out the windshield, I could see the snow falling again, see cars traveling in the rearview mirror back on the main road. Anyone could see us. All they would have to do was pull over. Notice my body jerking up and down. The car likely rocked some with my movements.

"Your pussy is like a tight fist, squeezing down on me. I just want to fucking pound into you," he growled, his hands leaving my breasts to grasp my hips. He aided my movements, shoving into me from below until we both groaned with the pleasure of it.

"Fuck—" My orgasm hit me hard, and my inner muscles contracted tightly on his tunneling cock. The waves of pleasure continued as he thrust into me with growling grunts of desperation until the final, grinding thrust before I collapsed back against his chest.

The windows were fogging up as we sat in the quiet stillness of the afternoon. Curled up half naked against his chest, one of my hands rested over his shoulder, fingers idly tracing the delineation of prominent muscles. He wasn't puffed up like a bodybuilder, but it was clear that he lifted weights, kept himself fit. One of his big hands cupped my inner thigh while the other played through the long strands of my hair splayed over his chest.

"I want to take you out. Officially. I know you're finishing up your doctoral work down in L.A., and that you live out by the beach. I'm living and working out of Pasadena. It's not that far. We can begin spending time together.

"Mmhmm," I said noncommittally, although my heart started pounding. That comfortable, relaxed, in-between time, the drifting on the good feelings time, was cut short. He wanted to make plans, put word to action. Irritation welled. I wasn't ready. We'd just had fun. Why couldn't he leave it at that?

"I want to see where this goes," he added, studying my face.

"I'm getting cold," I answered in a non-response. My tone was short. I'd meant to keep it even. Pulling away from his warm chest, I pulled my bra back down. He tried to help by pulling my bunched-up sweater back down, but I involuntarily snapped, "I've got it."

"What is this?" he frowned. "Why are you being this way?"

"What way? We had fun. It's getting cold. I want to head back to where it's warm."

"So that's how you want to play it? Okay. Be gutless. Let's pretend I'm just like every other guy who just wants to fuck you and leave. Let's pretend you aren't one of my closest friends, who I love. Let's fucking pretend that I'm a shitbag, so you don't have to think about this scary new place you find yourself in."

"Stop it! That's not what I'm trying to do."

"Isn't it?"

Shoving back against him, I pulled my pants back up and scrambled back over the gear shift to the other seat. "No! It's just freaking me out!"

"You think I'm impervious to having my heart broken? You think this isn't scary to me?"

"And this is why we shouldn't do this!"

"Why?"

"Because I don't want to be responsible for your heart. You deserve someone better than me, someone who would know what to do, someone who knows how to be caring. I don't and I can't."

"You think things will be better if I have another woman instead of you? That it will make things better? When we have get-togethers at the holidays, you're okay with another woman making a claim on me? If that's the truth, then you're right. I want someone who'll fight for me just once in this fucking life."

He zipped up his pants and turned away from me, his face slipping into its all-business expression.

"Topher, I didn't mean—"

"I know what you meant. I'm not worth the risk for you. I get it. We had fun. We'll be friends. It's all good." He turned the key in the ignition, and the engine came to life. The heater kicked on, but the warm air couldn't take away the chill that had suddenly surrounded us.

"It's not like that."

"Get your seatbelt on," he sighed, keeping his eyes trained out the front windshield, but I could still see the sadness there.

I'd hurt him, but I didn't know how to make this better. I didn't know what I wanted, did I? Maybe time to think wasn't a bad idea. Imagining some other woman holding his hand, being more trusted to hear his secrets, hearing that sexy, hissing sound when he was being pulled thick and rigid from his pants, was enough to make me feel angry and sad at the same time.

I wanted to be his person in a way that I'd never wanted to with anyone else. It felt more real than anything else ever had before, and that was the reason I was so scared. Allowing this to happen would absolutely change my life.

Was I all right with that?

Chapter 7
Topher

I should have known better than to let my feelings show.

Workout. That's what I needed. Hit the slopes again and lose myself in exercise. Swing and a miss. That was what I had to own. Risks could come with rewards, but they could also come with loss.

"You aren't parking?" she asked, snapping her head my way when I merely pulled up to the curb and left the motor idling.

"I'm not ready to play nice just yet." My reply was short and to the point. "I'm going to burn off some steam. Maybe do a few more runs. The lift passes are still good for a few more hours. We paid for the full day." I still wasn't looking at her. I didn't want to see what she was feeling. It was better not knowing. It was better to go back to the way things were.

"I'll go with you."

"Look," I finally swung my gaze over to her, "you aren't responsible for my feelings. We're going to be okay." Somehow. It was hard to stomach the realization that I'd had the girl of my dreams for the grand total of maybe two hours.

"Come inside. You wanted to talk. Let's talk."

"Not now."

"Truth or dare?"

"Really?" I glared at her.

"Yeah, really."

"Fine," I grumbled, narrowing my eyes at her. "Truth."

"Truth?" That surprised her. I'd meant for it to. She'd expected me to carry on the same way we'd been doing, but I was done with the novelty. I wanted to know what was in her heart and mind.

"The truth." She looked down at her hands that were tightly clasped together, took a deep breath and closed her eyes. "The truth is I've always had a thing for you, but I always made sure to keep distance between us."

"Why?"

"Because I knew that being with you would be different from every other relationship I'd ever been in. I knew that with you—" She looked up at me and held my gaze for a brief moment, pale eyes clinging to mine, begging me to understand. "—my life would have to change. I'd have to be real. This could be real. Being with you, well, it would be a moment of reckoning where you would either accept me or reject me for being what I am."

"See, I still don't understand what you're saying here. What exactly do you think you are?"

"I'm damaged." Her eyes shimmered with moisture that she blinked away. "I'm not respectable. I'm not good for anyone."

"Why the fuck would you say that?"

"It's what my stepmother told me when she found out about the club." She glanced down at her lap again.

"You told her?"

"Lucian did. After I'd taken him there."

Bastard. What a prick. I needed to kick the crap out of that motherfucker.

"He told my stepmother that I'd let three men fuck me, and that there was no way he could be with me. She asked if that was true, and I told her it was, at which point I was slapped for the second time that night. Told me to leave and have no contact with her or my half-sister."

"The second time?" I frowned.

"Lucian had slapped me first. At the club. Remember?"

"What the fuck? That was literal?" Fury pumped hot and fast through my blood. I'd missed that. I should have beat the shit out of him. It had to happen.

"Thinking he had some leverage, he also told her that he would leave. Stop working the vines and production if he didn't get shares in the company—now that my father was dead. At that point I calmly informed all of them, since they didn't seem to know any better, that the vines and the house were all mine, having belonged to my mother's family. I owned all of it. If I wanted to, I could kick all of them the hell out."

"Did you?"

"No. My step-sister is a sweetheart, and she lived there while she went to school. I told Lucian he could kiss my ass, that I would simply hire someone recommended by the family we still have in France where our sister vineyard thrives. He could fuck right off. Then I left. I haven't talked with my stepmother since, but my sister and I still talk. Every so often, Lucian makes contact. Pretends to care. He still hopes to have a piece of the pie. Not going to happen."

"Let's go inside," I sighed, noticing that her hands had a tremor to them. She was cold and emotional. And I wasn't sure what she wanted with me. We were in a strange place.

"You'll come, too?" Her eyes were wet. She was pleading with me, and there was no way I could ever say no to this girl.

"Yes."

The fire was going, creating a warm, welcoming feel. Soft holiday music came from speakers mounted in the ceiling, and the smell of spices and roasting beast clung to the air. Competing with the holiday sounds was the roar of the crowd on TV.

College football was on, and I was glad to have something to keep me occupied since Seth and Connor were doing their dance around the kitchen and refused any offers of help. With a sigh, I collapsed back beside the arm of the sofa. Simone disappeared, which left me wondering what we were going to do now. I didn't have to wait long. When she returned from her room, I drank in her beauty, and I didn't mean her physical appearance.

Of course, I couldn't help but notice that. My dick could get hard just knowing she was in the same room. It could get hard just seeing her car pull up. It didn't take much, and it was always a struggle. Added to that, I now knew what she looked like when she came. I knew what she tasted like.

She lingered by the kitchen area. She'd pulled off her snow pants, keeping her leggings on, and I couldn't help but wonder if she'd put her panties back on.

It was probably best not to go there. She wasn't looking for what I was looking for. Still, I couldn't help but check out her ass with a quick glance over my shoulder, looking to see if there were any panty lines visible. Hard to tell. If I slid my hand down the front of her leggings, would I get to feel that center of warm, wet heat again?

Fuck.

I adjusted as my pants grew tight in the crotch.

"What can I do?" Simone asked the guys. Because it was an open-concept house, the main rooms were a mash up, one blurring into the next for functionality.

"I need you to go keep our boy company," Connor answered. "I need you to loaf. Be lazy. If we need you, we'll call you."

"You asked for it," she chuckled. "I can do that." It was then she came back into my periphery, scooted around the other side of the sofa, eyed me for a beat, and dropped down next to me.

My attention was caught by the full bounce of her tits. God damn. Was she trying to kill me? It didn't look like she wore a bra anymore. I could yank that shirt up and have my lips around her gorgeous nipples in the next moment.

But she only wanted to fuck. I didn't want to just

be a fuck buddy. She meant more to me than just that. She'd poured her heart out in the car. I wanted her to know that it meant something to me.

Clearing my throat, I leaned closer to her, not wanting the guys to hear. "If I ever see that guy again, I'm going to beat his ass for you."

"You want to beat his ass?" she asked, her eyes going wide.

"Anyone who hurts you." I meant it.

Her eyes shimmered again, but then her hand was on my thigh, squeezing. It was likely a gesture of thanks, but my cock jerked at the proximity. But then she slid closer to me, moved her hand up my leg. Glancing at her, I saw her eyes were back on the game. She didn't know she was starting a party in my pants I was going to have to quash.

Then her hand moved again. It was so close, her pinky finger touching the straining bulge. I gritted my teeth and covered her hand. "You're killing me, Simone."

"What happened to calling me Lips?"

"I know you aren't sure what you want here, but I know I want to be more than your fuck buddy."

"What if I want more, too."

"What are you saying?" I was surprised by her words and my grip lessened. In the next moment, her hand was over my cock, squeezing its painfully hard length. I barely bit back the hiss of pleasure, it felt so good.

"More. Of you. Of us."

"Define that." I covered her hand where it gripped me through my pants, but I didn't pull her away.

"We try this. Us. I won't lie. It scares the crap out of me." Her eyes were shadowed with vulnerability. "But I trust you enough to try and be real with you."

Hearing her words sent a wave of happiness and relief tumbling through my body. It was all I wanted. I wanted the opportunity for us to grow. To be nurtured. To happen. I knew we could make this work, given the chance. There was no other woman who had ever taken the spotlight in my life.

Giving her hand a squeeze around my cock, I whispered, "Go up to my room and get naked. Last door at the end of the hall."

"You don't want to watch the game?"

"Oh, there's a game all right. Truth or dare?"

"Dare."

"I dare you to show me how you fingered yourself on that beach in Hawaii."

Her eyes grew heated. Her breath caught.

"Yes."

"You see, Lips, you're not damaged. You're dirty. And I love my dirty girl."

Chapter 8
Simone

It was embarrassing how wet I was already.

Anything to do with my big, muscular, glasses-wearing nerd, even just thinking about him, was fuel for arousal. His deep voice telling me what to do could almost have me coming spontaneously. There was freedom in feeling like I didn't have to hide who I was.

By the time I was naked, I'd decided to keep it simple. Sitting demurely in the messy covers he'd left that morning, his sheets smelling faintly of his soap and of him, was challenging. Only my breasts were fully visible, and when he came in, he paused after closing the door behind him. His eyes moved over me in a deliberate caress. My nipples peaked and a fresh shiver of awareness brought goosebumps to my flesh.

"Sitting naked in my bed, waiting for me, is exactly where you should be." He narrowed his eyes, kept them on me while finding his way to the armchair facing the foot of the bed. Stretching his legs out, the bulge in his pants prominent, he commanded, "Now show me."

I was determined to make him feel as crazy as he made me feel. Leaning back against the mound of pillows, I languidly licked my middle finger before drawing a line down my chest, over my nipple, something that made me moan, and down toward the bare folds of my pussy.

Then I opened my legs wide, feeling decadent.

Casting a look in Topher's direction, I saw him run a hand over his cock, squeezing it. I purred, "Pull it out. I want to see it."

A faint smile curled his lips before he unzipped his pants and pulled his thick, jutting cock out. "Is this what you want?"

It was beautiful, and I wanted to get it in my mouth, but I'd made promises.

"On the beach that day, when the other couple was going at it, I started out by rubbing my clit. It was hot and swollen, just like now." My fingertips ran over my sensitive slit that throbbed and became more swollen the longer I sat there. The moan was spontaneous, trembling between my lips on a shaky breath as I watched his eyes grow darker with intent.

"Did you put your fingers inside yourself?" he asked.

"Yes." I moved my middle finger through my dripping arousal and pushed it up into myself, curling it to massage my wall. My hips moved immediately, triggered to fuck, to accept the delicious invasion, the pressure against walls of my pussy. My head tilted back on a moan.

"Fuck, that's hot," Topher groaned. "I could watch you all day. So fucking beautiful. Add another finger." His tone had gone rougher, deeper, more primal.

I pushed another finger in, gasping with the pleasure of feeling fuller. I was starting to pant as the heat ramped up. Tilting my head back up, I made eye contact, letting him see the raw need, the desperate search for release. I moved my fingers just a little faster, in and out, gasping each wave of pleasure, before pulling my own juices up to my clit to rub some more.

"I'm close," I panted, slowing the movement of my fingers. "I want to come with you inside me. Please," I ended on a hiss, my body vibrating with the need to come, my hips still undulating.

I met him at the side of the bed on my knees, reaching for his cock. It was finally going to be mine. The moment my tongue lapped at the precum on his tip, I felt his groan vibrate through my body. Sucking him all the way in, I covered as much of his length as I could handle, practically choking on him. The sounds he was making, his tortured "fuck" comments that he hissed out, were my own private aphrodisiac, causing my arousal to drip down my inner thighs.

Then he pulled out and tossed me back onto the bed before crawling up between my legs. Somewhere between me sucking his dick and him settling his weight on me, he'd shed his clothes: stepped out of boots, yanked the thermal from his back over his head, and shoved his pants and boxers down his legs.

Then we were kissing, and the kisses changed. He was changing things. They became slower, deeper, more tender. Nibbles and kisses on my neck, a hand that mapped my rib cage, hip bone, and outer thigh, finding the sensitive spot behind my knee that even I didn't know about.

"What are you doing?" I whispered as a shiver worked through me.

"Showing you how much you mean to me." He stared down at me when he said that, and I knew I could happily drown in his eyes.

All of him. All of us. I made a decision. This would be a first for me.

"I want you to come inside me. I want to feel you there. I'm on the pill, and I've never let someone go bare before, so I'm clean."

"I'm clean, too. I never go bare."

"It'll be a first for both of us."

Then he slid home, and we were skin to skin. It wasn't just fucking. It was making love.

The slice of air between our lips held our moans secret. My legs went around his hips, and my arms ran over the muscles in his back, holding him close. We stared into each other's eyes when he began to move, and reflected there was the promise he was making—that I was it for him. Seeing that promise brought tears to my eyes.

"I want to make you come over and over again." He picked up the pace. "I want to watch you come for the rest of our lives."

"Yes," I cried, meeting each of his thrusts, working with him as sensation built on sensation. "I want to make you crazy for me, and only me. I want that."

"Already done." He ran a hand down my thigh to cup my ass before he pulled me deeper into his thrusts. Then his mouth was on mine again, his tongue sweeping inside, caressing mine, as his hips pumped and ground in a sensual move that had me whimpering with each stroke.

"Please," I broke away to gasp. It was all I could say, but it was all I needed to say.

"I'll take care of you, Lips." He moved his hand from my ass to my clit, pressing and rubbing as he began pounding into me. Harder. Faster. And then I jerked against him when the final tsunami hit.

"Topher!" I cried and felt him thrust and grind one more time on a growling shout of his own. His cum seared as it coated the inside of my pussy. He was still thick and pulsing, setting off more delicious ripples of contractions through my abdomen. We held on to each other through the pleasure of it all.

There was no one else I'd ever wanted to hold on to so badly and never let go.

He was it for me.

Epilogue
One Year Later

Topher

"Sex in hotel rooms is hot," Simone sighed, casting a wistful side eye toward our rumpled sheets.

"Don't," I smirked, even though my cock liked the idea of going another round, "or we'll be late, and you're the maid of honor."

"Not if we're quick."

Her dress was a lime sheath with spaghetti straps, material that cupped her breasts and outlined her shapely body, stopping mid-thigh. She'd thrown her hair up into an elegant bun that left a lot of skin around her neck and shoulders bare. Her expression was a mix of mischief and arousal.

Beautiful. Sexy. Hot. Brilliant.

I was the luckiest bastard alive to have this woman, and I was never going to get tired of playing with her, living with her, being partnered with her. She'd moved into my place not long after our time at the cabin. I found I couldn't live without her. I didn't want to wake up without having her by my side even one more day and was relieved when she said she felt the same way.

"What if I told you I wasn't wearing any underwear?" She tilted her head with a coquettish smile.

That got my attention. My eyes scanned her dress, looking for signs. It was hard to tell, but the idea alone had me going from zero to sixty in a millisecond. Now I had to know.

"Show me," I commanded.

"Find out for yourself."

Casually, suddenly not giving a shit that we were going to be late, I strolled to the small work/dining table where Simone had been gathering her phone and purse. Never losing eye contact, I saw the moment she felt my hand on her inner thigh. The small parting of her lips as she skipped a breath, waiting to see what I would do. Her eyes grew heavier. Dilated.

My fingers worked up the hem of her dress as they skimmed soft, silky skin until I felt the material of her panties.

"You're a tease, Lips," I observed in an even voice, not removing my fingers from where they were. Sliding under the edge of the lacy material I'd encountered, I stroked the wet, swollen flesh that awaited my invasion. "You just wanted to get me going, didn't you?"

"Yes," she breathed out, shakily.

"So that means, I need to leave a load right in here." I showed her where by sliding my fingers inside her sweet pussy.

She moaned, nodding, closing her eyes with the sensation, whispering, "Yes."

"Turn around. Hands on the table," I commanded, knowing how much she loved being told what to do and being physically manhandled. We both got off on it. Already the excitement was winding up the tension, promising an end worth being late for.

She turned, grasped the table, and watched me over her shoulder as she bent over. Gently, so as not to ruin the dress, I pulled the delicate material up over her hips, noting that she wore a white thong with sexy lacing. But best of all, a tiny little bell hung on a short satin ribbon. Fuck. Me.

I tapped it, knowing it would call to me all night long.

"You better hold on, Lips. I'm about to give you a quick ride."

It didn't take long to unzip, take out my heavy length, push the soaked lace aside, and rub my dick through her dripping arousal. In no time, I was slick enough to push through her swollen folds clear to the base of my cock, both of us groaning with the exquisite sensation. I gave us a beat or two to feel it, to run my hands down her arms and over her fingers where they gripped the edges of the table, but this wasn't the time to savor.

"You," I pulled out and pushed into her with a sharp move that made the desk knock into the wall, "are a naughty woman." I shoved into her again. Her sharp cry ended with a mewling whimper.

"More," she pleaded. "Faster."

The sound of skin slapping skin and hoarse cries filled the room from the moment I let go. Grasping her hips, I was rough, hard, plowing into her sweet, hot little pussy over and over again.

The phone rang, and from above her, I could see that it was Cat, likely wanting to know where we were.

"Answer it," I growled, not slowing, in fact shoving into her a little harder and a little faster until the desk rhythmically pounded into the wall. I gave no fucks about who was on the other side of it.

Sliding a shaky finger across her screen, she picked up her cell and put it to her ear.

"Yes?" She tried to keep her voice even as I tried

to make her unravel. "Doing? Uh… Running late? Yes." I reached a hand around to pinch and rub at her clit, and her breath hitched, her tone reaching a higher pitch when she said, "Be right there. I'm coming…" And then she did.

She gasped out a cry at the same time her pussy clamped down on my cock in a silken fist, but I didn't let up. I kept a steady rub on the fleshy nerves as I pounded half a dozen more times to my own guttural release. It was all I could do to keep us upright, clinging to the desk. I was draped over her, still filling her, clamped as deeply as I could go, both of us gasping for breath.

This was my life. She was going to be mine for as long as she would have me, and it was time to make that legal.

"Are you guys done yet?" came the faintly heard, amused female voice from Simone's phone. She hadn't hung up. "I mean, it's only my wedding, right? Don't fuck up the dress. We're doing pictures after. Now get dressed and help me get married."

Simone gaped up at me over her shoulder before we both started cracking up.

Needless to say, we took a lot of heat before and after the wedding. It took place on Beck's father's estate just outside San Francisco, with close family and friends. Being a foster child most of his life, his family had found him only the year before, and that had turned into a beautiful thing. The family resemblance was obvious between him, his father and his two brothers, though not so much his sister, who resembled her mother. Beck's father had met and married a lovely woman after having a short fling with Beck's mother. With the addition of his father's family, he'd gained a few aunts, uncles, cousins, and a set of grandparents who still teared up with emotion when they looked at him. Beck was finally having the life he'd always wanted, particularly with Cat by his side.

Not that he hadn't had the five of us as his family for the last few years. We were a self-created family, one of the strongest kind. We'd chosen each other, and because of that, Beck's family had taken us all on. There were already plans, not only for the six of us at the cabin for some skiing, but for all of us with Beck's family when it was holiday time again. We were now one big happy family—almost. There was still one more thing I had to do.

"Aren't you guys tired?" Beck's father asked as the final guests left.

"Actually, now that you mention it..." Simone covered a yawn, but Beck, Cat, Seth, and Connor were already leading the way down to the rock-covered beach. She arched a brow of confusion after them, but then she followed. The moon was full, making it unnecessary to bring any other light.

She frowned, tossing me a glance over her shoulder, but picked her way down the sandy path.

"It's a beautiful night sky," I explained at her questioning look. "We won't be here to enjoy it tomorrow night."

"That's true," she nodded and continued down the path.

When the sand became too much for her shoes, I helped her take them off before picking her up and carrying her the rest of the way down the sand. Beck had grabbed Cat and thrown her over his shoulder, deciding to jog down the beach with her threatening to puke up dinner on his jacket.

They had done it. Now it was our turn.

Pausing at the edge of the tide pools, I set her down carefully, making sure she had her feet under her.

"Look up at the moon," I whispered in her ear.

She turned to look up at the sky and sighed. "It looks so big."

"Didn't you say that to me the first time we—" I hugged her close, her back to my front.

"Topher!"

"Well, you did."

I felt the others coming to surround us. The perfection of the moment couldn't be replicated, and the warmth and tenderness radiating from my heart told me now was the time. When I took a quick look over my shoulder, I saw my family smiling their excitement, their encouragement.

"It's a beautiful night," Simone sighed, not realizing that our friends were gathered behind us.

I pulled the ring box out of my pocket.

Seth reached over to squeeze my shoulder in support before slinging his arm back around Connor, who looked like he was about to tear up. Cat gave me a thumbs' up while Beck kissed the top of her head, looking like he was a man on top of his world. I took a deep breath. It was time to begin our future.

I stepped back and knelt at her feet. Feeling the sudden chill, she looked over her shoulder and, seeing me at her feet holding a ring, she gasped. A hand flew to her chest like she was keeping her heart from jumping out.

"Topher?" There was a vulnerability to her words.

"I love you, Simone."

Tears were already welling up, slipping silently down her cheeks. She knelt in front of me. Her hands cupped my face. With her voice full of emotion, she said, "I love you, too."

I pulled one of her hands to my lips to kiss it before holding it between my own.

"I wanted to bring you out here in front of our friends, with the wild sound of the crashing waves and the moon rising high, to tell you how I feel about you. People have sat here listening to the waves and staring up at the same moon since the beginning of time, and it occurred to me I want to be staring up at that moon with you for my whole life. I want to marry you. I want to have crazy monkey sex with you. I want to worry over kids' grades with you. I want to grow old with you. And one day, when my time is done, I want to be looking into your eyes when I fade out. Marry me, Simone. Let's have a wonderful, outrageous, normal, crazy life together."

She was nodding before I could finish my last words.

"I didn't think I would ever be able to meet someone. I thought there was something wrong with me."

"There's nothing wrong with you. You're perfect."

"That's what I've learned. I'm perfect for you. And you're perfect for me. I couldn't do this with anyone else. It's you for me."

I took her hand and slid the ring home where it belonged.

It was my promise of forever.

***

Thank you for reading TRUTH OR DARE I hope you love Topher and Simone as much as I do. If you missed Beck and Cat's story, and you'd like to continue reading about what else happened that holiday weekend, find WINTER HEAT on Amazon, which is available now!

I'm thrilled to offer an excerpt of my new release ONE BREATH TO THE NEXT, a contemporary full-length novel about Layla and Mason, new, sexual awakening, and fighting a dark past to reach for a beautiful future.

Sign up for Danube Adele's NEWSLETTER to get updates on new releases at danubeadele.com.

Turn the page to read the first chapter of ONE BREATH TO THE NEXT.

One Breath to the Next

Excerpt: Chapter 1

CHAPTER 1

MASON

"Two more. Give me two more, Garcia. Do it now. Go." I used my no-bullshit voice despite the fact that my own teeth clenched in reaction to the pain etched on his face.

"I can't do it, Mason," Jay Garcia snarled through gritted teeth, even as he pulled the weights attached to what was left of his calves from his wheelchair. A guttural cry tore from his lips. His entire body shook with the effort and the agony. Sweat poured off him as the weights rose hesitantly to the top of the pulley and fell back, completing a rep.

"The fuck you can't. Two more," I replied, inches from his face, ignoring the swell of empathy that erupted from deep in my soul seeing the pool of moisture in his eyes. Jay had mountains to climb to meet his recovery potential.

"One more!" He growled, his eyes angry and slitted. If Jay could talk while he was pumping weights, he wasn't working hard enough.

"Three more!" I taunted him. "You can take a fucking bomb to the legs but you can't do three more reps?"

"Fuck you!" Jay roared. His dark eyes turned pink and glassy with shimmering moisture. It threatened to spill over. His legs jerked on the pulley again, his arms braced against his wheelchair. The shining stack of heavy steel rose halfway up the pulley, paused for a fraction of a second, then got yanked all the way up.

"Life isn't going to hand you a fucking trophy for effort, Garcia. Push yourself. Don't give up. Again. Go. Now."

"I'll fucking kill you," he groaned.

"When you can fucking walk again, I invite you to try, asshole. Now quit your whining and lift the fucking weights."

"Fuck you! Fuck you, motherfucker!" His face was red, and the veins in his neck and temple started to bulge. But lift the weights he did. Two more times in quick succession—like I knew he could—before he set the weights back with a heartfelt cry of release that came from somewhere deep in his barrel chest.

Shouts and applause erupted from the small crowd that had gathered to watch our training session, a few calls of congratulations sprinkled here and there before people went about their own workouts again. The tears that had been threatening streamed down Jay's cheeks as an emotional, hoarse sob ripped from the depths of his chest, making his large upper body shake with the force.

"Yes. You. Can." I clasped his forearm in a secure grip, locked eye contact, and crouched close by his wheelchair. "I got you, brother. I got you."

"I know it." He nodded, using his left hand to swipe at the moisture on his face. "I don't deserve it, but I know it."

"Bullshit. We all deserve it."

Jay shook his head as more tears dripped down his scruffy face. He had stopped shaving in the last week or so, refusing to accept care, and I knew why. In combat, when bad shit went down around you, it ended up becoming your living nightmare. It sank sharp, poisonous claws deep into your soul. Turned you into a beast, and when you looked into the mirror, you couldn't see yourself anymore.

Jay's demons were riding him hard. From the moment he'd come in this morning, I could see he'd had a bad night. Maybe he'd had several in a row, judging from the bags under his eyes. There was a new sense of fatigue clouding him, and that was dangerous. He wasn't giving his workout the same heart he'd started with a few months back.

"What's going on?" I asked. He knew what I was asking. He didn't even try to deflect.

"Tammy left." Jay swiped at his eyes. "She said I wasn't even trying anymore. Packed her shit and took off a couple of days ago."

Fuck. The worst time for it to happen. He'd been making progress. "Why would she say that?"

"We've been fighting for the last couple of months. She said it was like she was living with a stranger. It's been almost six months since I got back and nothing's changed. I don't talk to her anymore. I don't see her. Shit like that." He paused. His lips thinned into a tight line, like he was trying to control a well of emotion, and he sniffed sharply. Still, a few renegade tears fell down his cheeks. "I don't blame her. She deserves better."

I bit my tongue, refusing to say something negative about a woman who should have had the patience to let Jay readjust to not only civilian life after living in a fucking war zone, but also to now living life as an amputee, his legs missing from the knees down. He hadn't shared the details of how the bomb hit, but I was sure it was as fucked-up as the rest of the stories I'd heard from guys coming back, my own included.

I shook my head, my words quiet. "I'm sorry to hear that."

He sniffed, gave a final swipe to his eyes and hung his head. "Stopped taking the meds."

"Why?"

"They aren't doing any good. Can't fucking sleep anymore. Don't want to sleep."

"Nightmares?"

He nodded.

"You talking about your shit with someone?" I asked quietly. "There's all different kinds of therapies they could offer you. Other kinds of medicines that'll maybe work better."

The answer was already in his eyes when he looked back up at me, dark and grim. His jaw was set square, tensing when he gave a sharp jerk of his head.

"What the fuck, dude?" I shot out in a low voice, wanting to make sure the conversation stayed between us. "You need help. You can't deal with this on your own."

He could only shake his head. The fact he was starting to head down this path meant he was heading toward a fucking unacceptable conclusion. Too many soldiers had already taken their lives. There was no way I was giving up on Jay Garcia. I didn't know what visions haunted him at night, but I knew how they could fuck with a person. It had taken me years, but I'd finally made some inroads.

He wouldn't look me in the eye, and I knew what it was. Worse than the injury that had permanently changed the landscape of his body was the feeling of worthlessness and being unable to forgive himself. He'd done something he felt he couldn't live with. Just like me. That shit lived on a reel in your psyche just waiting for unguarded moments to hit play.

Like now.

Talking with Jay sparked the sharp memory of relentless heat under a desert sun. The heavy weight of my pack. Rivulets of sweat.

My breath caught in the back of my throat as I fought to smother the memory, tried to ignore it, swallow it down, and press on. I needed to make sure Jay was all right.

"Talk to me, Jay."

He shook his head a final time, took the brake off his wheelchair and pushed away. "I gotta go. I've got an appointment to get fitted for new prosthetics. Some high tech shit. I'm about to become the bionic man." He forced a carefree smirk.

I was relieved he was still going to the appointment. If he ever stopped coming to the gym or started skipping doctor visits, it would be time for an intervention on his ass. Until then, it was natural for him to go through the rollercoaster effect of ups and down. Recovery, both physical and emotional, took time. And it sucked that his girlfriend of the last two years had decided to jump ship.

I gave a quick nod, lightly clapped his shoulder, and stood. "That happening today?"

"Yeah." He paused as if a thought had just occurred to him.

"What?"

He looked like he wanted to say something, but then he shook his head. "Nothing."

"I hope you know if you need something, I'm here for you." There was so much he needed. I knew this, but his life was out of my control. There was nothing I could do but encourage, prod, badger… He wheeled himself out of the automatic glass door that led to the rest of the gym, and I prayed I wasn't watching a dead man taking his last breaths. I never wanted to see that again.

A sudden image lanced my heart. It was crystal clear. In vibrant color. Details sharply outlined in my mind.

Gasping breath. Gurgling blood. The sky reflected in wide blue eyes that slowly turned lifeless.

That's when it hit. I'd let myself go there. Let my mind pull up the bits of memory. Enough to get triggered. Always. My throat squeezed down, my chest banded tightly, and my heart beat like a wild thing trapped in a too-small cage trying to get free. Fuck me. Not now. My office was so far away. Across the entire fucking gym. I couldn't reach it.

I tried to relax, struggled to take a breath. Fought the tunnel vision starting to take over. It wasn't working. Instantly, I looked for my saving grace.

Where was she?

My gaze turned wild while I tried to maintain my cool. I looked through the glass walls out into the main gym area, searching for the girl who had the ability to calm me with a single glance. She was here. I'd already seen her. She was here every day. I moved through the sliding door and felt the wheezing start, the fight for a single breath. If I couldn't calm down soon, I was going to pass out.

She wasn't on a cardio machine. She wasn't using weight machines. She was by the free weights, standing perfectly still in front of the mirror, her tranquil indigo eyes already watching me. Captivating me. Our eyes locked. I fell into the endless pool of calm peacefulness reflecting back at me. She was a little thing. Fragile. Precious. Probably only came up to my shoulder, but she housed special powers that were far greater than her size.

Don't look away, I thought desperately, already feeling my chest ease.

I won't, she seemed to say, holding me up with a look.

Was it seconds or minutes later that I could take a deep breath again? Feeling foolish and vulnerable, I broke the connection. Moved with purposeful strides across the gym until I reached my office and closed the door, still breathing heavily. Dots of sweat coated my upper lip. My whiskers rasped as I wiped the back of my long-sleeve T-shirt along the moist skin, but I still didn't let her out of my sight. I brought up the security monitors on my computer screen, found her in the same spot. She was looking toward my office door, blotting sweat from her slender neck with one of the white towels we provided.

There was something about her that spoke to me, something gentle and pure. Innocent. Uncorrupted. Lacking in artifice. There was a warm, comforting energy about her that I was addicted to. As if she were on a frequency that connected to my soul and eased the chaos that bombarded me, yet we'd never had a single conversation. She was an angel. My own personal angel.

Her name was Layla.

Find ONE BREATH TO THE NEXT on
Amazon to get the story!

MORE BOOKS BY DANUBE ADELE

Kiss and Tell

Book 1: WINTER HEAT

Book 2: TRUTH OR DARE

Hermosa Beach Memoirs Series

Book 1: One Breath to the Next

Book 2: Fiery Blessing – preorder

ABOUT THE AUTHOR

Danube Adele believes that a good nap can solve most problems, diving into new adventure kickstarts creativity, and quiet walks along the beach soothe the soul. Add a mango margarita paired with chips and salsa to the mix, and you get a happy life. Author of the paranormal, sci-fi romance series Dreamwalkers, she can often be found either eagerly typing away at an HEA on her laptop, or lounging on the sofa with a hot, sexy romance novel in hand. She's lived in southern California her entire life, and much of that time with her greatest fans, her loving husband and two brilliant sons.

Sign up for Danube's newsletter:

www.danubeadele.com

Like Danube Adele on Facebook:

www.facebook.com/Writer.D.Adele

Manufactured by Amazon.ca
Bolton, ON

25437734R10081